MELT

a MUST READ. Bravo to Selene Castrovilla on writing one of the best books of 2014."

—Lady Reader's Bookstuff

"MELT … reminded me of why I love to read. My heart was literally pounding … I couldn't put it down."

—Eve's Fan Garden

"This is such a captivating read from the start. I got so involved with the characters that I was afraid to leave them, afraid that I might miss out on something big if I stop reading."

—The Cursed Empire

"I get the writing style of MELT isn't for everyone. It's written as verse, poetic-like. But the book is so deep, but yet such an easy read. I'll never forget it. NEVER.

And I'll forever recommend it as a must-read. The fact that she could introduce these deep characters in such a structure and make me feel like I know them is mind blowing.

I have nothing but praise to the author … she created a powerful book that will forever hunts the reader. Poignant and entirely realistic, MELT is a book that should NEVER be missed."

—Her Book Thoughts!

"All I could think was 'God help them'. And I couldn't stop reading."

—Sheri's Reviews, Goodreads

"Different. Intense. Perfect.

This story was all of these, and so much more."

—Bibilophilia, Goodreads

For Agostina —
Follow your Yellow
Brick Road!
Enjoy!

MELT

Selene Castrovilla (signature)

BY

SELENE CASTROVILLA

"Instantly the wicked woman gave a loud cry of fear, and then, as Dorothy looked at her in wonder, the Witch began to shrink and fall away.

'See what you have done!' she screamed. 'In a minute I shall melt away.'

'I'm very sorry, indeed,' said Dorothy, who was truly frightened to see the Witch actually melting away like brown sugar before her eyes.

'Didn't you know water would be the end of me?' asked the Witch, in a wailing, despairing voice.

'Of course not,' answered Dorothy. 'How should I?'"

—From *The Wonderful Wizard of Oz* by L. Frank Baum

Castrovilla, Selene
Melt / Selene Castrovilla. – 1st ed.
p. cm
Summary: Sixteen-year-old Dorothy meets seventeen-year-old Joey
in a Long Island doughnut shop, and struggles to save him from
alcoholism and nihilism, while Joey keeps a secret that threatens them
both: his police officer father abuses and terrorizes his family.

ISBN-10: 0991626117
ISBN-13: 978-0-9916261-1-3

[1. Young adult – Fiction. 2. Family problems – Fiction. 3. Domestic
violence – Fiction. 4. Alcoholism – Fiction. 5. Abuse – Fiction. 6.
Love – Fiction. 7. Bildungsroman – Fiction. 8. New York – Fiction.]

Cover Design by Damonza.com
Cover photo by Sarah Delk
Interior Design by Damonza.com
Edited by Evelyn Fazio
Copyedited by Jenny Peterson

Printed in the USA
10 9 8 7 6 5 4 3 2 1

First Edition

BOOKS BY SELENE CASTROVILLA

By the Sword

Melt

Revolutionary Friends

Saved by the Music

The Girl Next Door

Upon Secrecy

❧

Selene is pleased to have a piece included in the charitable
book anthology

Travel in the Sixties,

whose proceeds fund art/music therapy for
Alzheimer's patients.

For Joe Donovan

Thanks to my friends, who have been life support over the years. Thanks to my fans, whose connection with my work has provided me with satisfaction and happiness beyond all conceptions. Thanks to my sons, who give me joy, unconditional love and latitude when I'm writing.

No Place Like Home

"'What shall we do?' asked the Tin Woodman.
'If we leave her here she will die,' said the Lion."

—From *The Wonderful Wizard of Oz* by L. Frank Baum

Mom stopped crying a
long
time ago.
Now
she don't even
whimper
when he does it. He comes
home
in his steel blue shirt shiny black shoes shiny tie clip shining
badge
he blows in and the screen door
slams
behind him like it's pissed off
he's
back.
He comes in shuts the front door clicks the lock closed
he wipes his shoes on the mat

back and forth

back

and

forth he pads across the shit-brown carpet without a sound

his eyes are empty his eyes are

dark his eyes are

wrought

lead like his

Glock.

      I catch a whiff of his favorite mouthwash

Jack

Daniel's

he used to smell of Listerine and Jack but he don't bother trying

to

cover

up

these days.

Without a look he goes past me and Jimmy and Warren. Warren's

got his textbooks spread out across the couch but he ain't studying

not

no more. Grim music drifts from our video game low

chilling

sounds like any second the reaper's gonna

strike. Me and Jimmy we're playing *Halo* on Xbox, least we were

'til

he

came

back. It's like we're paused

we're all on

pause whenever
Pop
comes
home.
We ain't putting down the controls 'cause if we look at him if we
act like we're paying attention to what he's doing then he
might
come
after
us
next.
The freakish *Halo* music plays on and
on and
on. He heads through the arch to the kitchen his shoes
stamping on the green
linoleum he goes right over to
her
at the stove cooking his goddamn mashed potatoes stirring
stirring
stirring she don't move don't run she just stirs
stirs
stirs
he says
nothing
to her to the
girl he married to the
mother
of his kids he comes behind her at the stove
his shoes squeak he

grabs

her

the spoon plops in the potatoes no not even a plop not a sound it

sinks soundless

like

her.

He holds her against him blue sleeve on white apron

squeezing

squeezing

squeezing into her ribs like he's doing the Heimlich

his tie clip presses in her back

he sticks his semi-automatic piece of crap weapon in her mouth

clanks

it against her teeth shoves

it

down

her

throat clicks

off the safety and she don't

make a sound

she

just

stands there and takes it. Not a peep not a flinch not a blink of

panic

nothing she just takes it she

melts

for him

melts like the butter she stirred in his mashed potatoes made from

scratch

peeled one by one
eyes carved out
she
melts she just disappears
she's
gone.
Like every husband in the world kisses his wife like this.
Like she
deserves
it like she did something that'd
make
it
okay
for the man who
swore
to
love and cherish her
to do
this
in front of
me.
> Hey, I saw the video.
There wasn't nothing in those vows 'bout guns or fists neither
for that matter. Do you Caitlyn Ruby Shields promise to take
a pounding anytime Joseph Thomas Riley damn well feels like
laying one on? No, I don't think Father Gallagher mentioned that.
God I
hate
that name I

hate that I'm
named
after
him. My pop I mean. Not Father Gallagher.
     Mom in her satin white dress with the lacy veil and the
puffed
sleeves the long
train
dragging
behind her the big-ass bouquet of white roses she
cradled
in her arms
poor
Mom she looked so happy no one told her 'bout the guns. And
him
he's standing there by Father Gallagher in his black tux black
bow-tie
that
prick
he's always
so neat
looking
so smug
hair slicked
back I could've killed him even then if
only
I was born.
     That's a
lie

I can't even

kill

him

now.

I just sit here

pretending

to

play

Halo while my mom gets a Glock rammed down her throat I can't

even save my mom from this piece of shit who goes out to serve

and

protect

all day

some

joke.

       She stopped crying like five years ago.

       She stopped crying when I was twelve.

       Me I never cried much not in front of him he warned me

not to.

He told us me and my brothers not to let one tear drop on the

carpet or we'd get it too. He don't hit us much he just

says

he might.

Me and Jimmy we're pussies I guess Warren's nine what could he

do but me and Jimmy we sit there

day

after

day fingers touching stupid useless buttons day after

day night after

night he hits her hits
her hits
her and we watch.
Week after
week month
after month we
watch.
She gets slammed
into walls so hard pictures fall she gets shoved
so rough his finger marks are in her arm she gets thrown
to the floor and kicked
kicked
kicked
and we hold our controls and we hold our breaths and watch we
watch
we watch.

       Warren cries in bed. I check on him before I go to sleep,
stick my head in his door. The blankets are pulled up over him
he's just a
lump
underneath. There's no noise but the covers shake he's under there
holding it
all
in
I know 'cause I did that too.
He's only nine.
He'll learn to cut that shit
soon
enough.

Me and Jimmy we don't cry.

And she don't cry neither.

So

what's the

problem maybe this is

normal maybe this is

life maybe everybody on Long Island does this behind the doors

they close and lock when they come

home.

This's all I know and

maybe

this's right but it

don't feel right I wanna help her

but

I

don't.

I watch Mom suck steel and then we all eat. We sit at the

table slide our chairs in

we pick up our forks

like

nothing.

Pass the potatoes.

PART ONE
<u>MUNCHKINLAND</u>

"She was awakened by a shock, so sudden and severe that if Dorothy had not been lying on the soft bed she might have been hurt. As it was, the jar made her catch her breath and wonder what had happened; and Toto put his cold little nose into her face and whined dismally. Dorothy sat up and noticed that the house was not moving; nor was it dark, for the bright sunshine came in at the window, flooding the little room. She sprang from her bed and with Toto at her heels ran and opened the door."

—From *The Wonderful Wizard of Oz* by L. Frank Baum

One

DOROTHY

He looks like a sculpture by Michelangelo. Like his body was intricately carved, chip by chip until it was perfect.

He's beautiful.

When I saw his muscles—even half covered by his Metallica T-shirt they couldn't be denied—when I saw his arms, I knew they could keep me safe. Funny, I never thought I needed protection, but there it was, that thought, and just like that everything changed.

He was sitting with a bunch of guys in Dunkin' Donuts when Amy and I walked in. Dunkin' Donuts is apparently the mecca of teen society in Highland Park. Not that there's much to choose from in this one-square-mile town. There's a pizza place, a Chinese restaurant, a laundry … well, you get the picture. Manhattan, it's not. Anyway, the cool crowd gathers in Munchkinland.

Personally, I find the bright fuchsia and orange colors a tad aggressive on the eyes, but what the hey. When in Rome …. And it looks like I'm going to be in Rome for a while.

So Amy—the one friend I've made thus far in my two days here—she headed right past all those guys, just ignored them and headed for the counter. I meant to follow, but those biceps … they held me back.

Imagine if they were holding me.

The rest of the guys, they were yammering away, making crude jokes and cracking themselves up. He sat slightly apart, leaning his wrought iron chair back against the oh-so-pink wall.

My eyes scanned higher, rising over his thick, strong neck to his finely chiseled jaw, lips, cheeks, nose.

He's a work of art.

To his eyes then, to his smoky-grey eyes that stared back at me. He had the look of an animal caught in a trap. It was like he was caged inside that beautiful body, like he was asking me to carve deeper and set his soul free.

"What are you doing, Dorothy?"

I guess I didn't answer fast enough because Amy grabbed at my arm, pulled me closer to the counter. "Those guys, they're jerks. We don't talk to them."

"I wasn't actually talking to …."

"Listen, they're losers. Get your donut and come in the back room, that's where everyone is."

I turned and looked at him. He was still watching me, tracking me with those eyes ….

"Are you insane?" Amy yanked me around again. "That's Joey Riley. He's the biggest loser of them all."

"He doesn't look like a loser."

"Hel-*lo*, do you think losers come with big 'loser' signs attached? No, they can come in some exceptional packaging. But when you unwrap them and you peel away all that plastic coating stuff and rip off the safety tags, then guess what, it's too late to return them."

"Could you be more specific?" I asked.

"How about Joey Riley beats people up for fun, sends them to the hospital. How about Joey Riley drinks and smokes weed. How about Joey Riley's been arrested, sent to jai— Oh, crap, he's coming over .... Hey, Joey! What's up?" Amy's lips widened into a faux smile. I was beginning to not like my only friend. Maybe it was time to make another.

I turned around, faced him.

Faced those muscles, faced those eyes. If Amy was correct about him fighting he must've been awfully good, because he didn't have a visible mark. I tried to think of him as bad; I tried to shut him down in my head, but who was I kidding? He didn't answer Amy, he didn't even glance at her. He was all about me, and it was reciprocal.

"Hi, Doll," he said in a voice low and husky.

"Doll?" I echoed. "Are we in some sort of 1940s gangster movie?"

"What? No, I ... I didn't mean anything by ...." His face tensed, reddened.

"It's okay," I jumped in. "Doll should be the worst name I'm ever called."

His jaw loosened, and he smiled just a little, around the edges. "Haven't seen you around before," he said.

"I just moved here, from New York."

He nodded, his long brown hair brushing ever so slightly against his shoulders. Lucky hair. "That's cool. I'm Joey."

He hesitated, then offered me his hand. It was calloused,

kind of bent and bumpy-looking. His knuckles were uneven, bruised. I guessed he did punch people.

I hesitated, then took it.

A warm energy moved through me when we touched. It was all I could do not to melt into his arms, and I'm not the melting type.

I swallowed deeply. "I'm Dorothy."

JOEY

She looks like a
doll
like one of them
porcelain
dolls something so
fragile and
precious
you should put
high
on
a
shelf to keep
safe and never
never
touch.
Mom had a bunch of them three shelves full 'til Pop had
enough
he said he couldn't stand them all
staring
while he was sleeping.
And he didn't want
me
and
Jimmy near no girly shit neither he said
no sons
of his
were gonna

wind

up

fags. So Mom had to

pack

them up she

wrapped

them in that

bubble stuff she

taped

the boxes

real

good

so no dust would get in and she

left

them in Grandma's

basement.

I still remember them I remember their

faces all

smooth and delicate their

eyes so

wide so innocent like

nothing bad's

ever

happened

to them. Pure that's it they were

so

pure.

     She's like that.

     Hey

Doll,
I said that's what I
called her
without even thinking.
I almost didn't go over there she was with frigging Amy Farber her
crowd
don't
see
me
even when they see me. But she had those big blue eyes like my
mom's dolls so I went.
       She said something 'bout
the
movies
I didn't know
what
she was talking about. I thought
she was pissed but
then
she smiled
and
it
was
okay.
       Her hair's like those dolls' too.
Long and glossy.
And wavy.
It's wavy
like you could just

unfurl

your fingers in it and set course.

        You could just drift far

far away.

        There was all this noise in there. There was people

yakking on line ordering

donuts and shit

there was registers ringing there was tip

cups clinking

there was background music some kind of top forty whining b.s.

but when we started talking there was

only

our voices.

        She's new

here

she's from New

York, she said. You could tell she had class she was wearing a top

that actually fit her it

covered her not like these girls who let their stomachs hang out all

over the place like that's

supposed to be attractive.

I must be

crazy even

talking to her, I thought. She's probably used to all these

rich

fancy

dudes but the way she kept

looking

at me

I thought, Well maybe ….

There was all these eyes

watching.

There was Jimmy and the guys at the table

there was

frigging

Amy

there was the people buying

donuts and shit there was the people

ringing

shit

up.

But when we looked at each other there was

only us.

So I introduced myself I didn't wanna

stick

out

my hand

partly 'cause it's a

disaster all twisted

up from fights and I thought

for

sure

it would spook her but also 'cause she looked like a

doll

like one of Mom's

dolls

and you

shouldn't

ever

touch

them

they might break.

      But I did it.

I

forced

myself

'cause that's what you're supposed to do

especially

when someone's from a place all classy and

polished

like New

York that's what they do there and anyway

I

can't

lie

I really did wanna do it, I wanted to

touch

her.

      And she took it.

      She

took

it.

      I thought she

wasn't

gonna but she slipped her

soft

soft

fingers round my
rough
scabby
hand.
       She
touched me she
touched me she touched
me
and something warm
crackled
through my body.
It didn't start in me it didn't start in her it started right between
our hands like two sticks rubbing
like some kind of
friction
we caused together.
       For sure I thought she'd
drop
my hand like a
hot
potato
and run right outta Dunkin' Donuts but
she didn't.
       She said
her name was
Dorothy
and I thought,
Where's

Toto? But thank god I kept my trap shut that time 'cause how
many chances

do

you

get

really before you're chalked up for the

jerk

you

are?

       We were still holding hands looking at each other I was
just glad I wasn't

drooling

or something I'm such a

doofus and then

fucking

Amy

cleared her throat

A-hem

and Dorothy

let

go.

       You coming or what, Amy asked her and she said

yes

she

was.

She said

nice

to meet

me and all that crap.

I figured,

That's

that.

She went to the counter and ordered a croissant and a

mocha latte for crying

out

loud. What made me think

someone

like

that

would like

someone

like

me?

Someone who'd pick a

croissant

over a bagel or a donut.

Someone willing to pay

three

times

the

price to have

foamy

milk

on her coffee.

She could have anything

she could have

anyone.

So

why
the
hell
would she ever want
me?
      I started heading to the guys. I stared straight at the
psychedelically
pink
wall tried not to catch their eyes 'cause defeat's hard enough
without having to
look your friends
in
the
face.
The smell of
brewing
lattes
was making me dizzy.
The white ceiling lights beamed
down
on my head
bright
bright
bright.
The noises in that place were
way
too
loud.
My Nikes

slipped across
pale smoke tile
I could barely lift my feet.
It was all I could do not to
shut my lids and
melt
right
into
the
gray.
      But then I heard
my
name.
      She called
my name
she called my name she
called
my
name.
      She called me
back over.
      So I
went.

Two

DOROTHY

It was hard enough coping with all those swarming emotions without Amy there watching. I mean, I knew how she felt about Joey, and her standing there was like an invasion of our privacy. And she kept shooting these looks at him, like he was a gob of gum someone smushed under one of the tables.

Even though I didn't know him, I wanted to shield him from her glare.

The crazy thing was, even though I didn't know him, I did.

I don't like gossip. Usually they've got it wrong, somehow. And even if they've got it right, it always sounds like a judgment on the person they're talking about, who's not invited to give his side of the story. On the surface it sounded like she was trying to warn me about Joey, but deeper, it was really that she needed people like Joey to put down, to make her feel better about herself. If he was bad, then she must be good. But things are never black and white like that.

When she broke in and asked if I was coming, it wasn't a question. There wasn't room for me to say no, not if I wanted to go meet everyone—everyone who counted, according to Amy.

I caved, without thinking. I said yes, I was coming, and kind of brushed him off.

I didn't mean to, but I did.

Standing at the counter waiting for my stuff, I looked back for him. But he wasn't watching me anymore. He was kind of slogging back to his table. His shoulders were slumped—those beautiful arms practically dragged at his side, and he moved so slowly ….

I couldn't bear it.

"Joey," I called out over the sounds of grinding coffee, "Hey, Joey, come back."

Amy made this tut-tutting sound. She said she'd be in the other room if I decided to come, and then she sashayed away the way some girls do when they're just too cool. Personally, I walk. I don't wiggle, strut, or even stroll. I make it my business to walk, period.

At that point I wasn't too broken up about Amy heading off.

I'm not that desperate.

Joey spun around with his shoulders straightened and his head held high. We locked eyes and he smiled that smile again, just a little, around the edges. He strutted back over the grey tiles.

Here's the thing about strutting. On guys, I like it. Guys need a certain something in their walk, it's part of who they are. On girls, it's just pretension. For guys, it's a necessity.

"Hey," he said when he got up close again. He was still smiling.

"Hey," I said, smiling back. I'd never felt so instantly comfortable with someone, but at the same time there was this great pressure pounding in my chest, telling me not to blow it somehow.

Truth is, I'd never had a boyfriend. I'd hung out with a few guys, gone to the movies and such, but I never felt any inclination to go further with them. There was never any connection. I kind of thought that connection stuff was something fabricated by Hollywood, or conjured up in people's minds—people who needed to believe that there was some soul mate out there waiting to complete them, because they couldn't bear the burden of completing themselves.

I wasn't looking for completion, but god it was nice to *feel*.

So there I was doing all this mental babbling but saying nothing to him. He was just watching me, wearing that little side smile, almost like he was listening to the thoughts inside my head. It would've creeped me out with anyone else, but with him, it was awesome.

He must've known that I was back in focus, because he said, "Wanna sit, or something?" He pointed to a table for two by the window, overlooking the parking lot.

"Sure," I said.

We sat, stared at each other some more, in a really cozy way.

Like they do in the movies.

Like I never thought could be, in real life.

I sipped my latte. "Want some?"

He shook his head no. "I don't do foam."

"Oh," I said.

He made a face like he couldn't believe he'd said that. "Uh, I mean …."

"It's fine. You don't do foam. I can respect that."

He laughed. He had such a great, deep laugh, and his eyes twinkled when he did it, like they were laughing too.

"So, are your parents into *The Wizard of Oz*? That why they named you Dorothy?"

"Actually, I'm named after Dorothy Parker." I pulled a piece of my croissant off and popped it in my mouth.

"Who's that?"

"She was a writer in the 1920s. She used to get together with a bunch of other literary types, hang out at the Algonquin."

He raised his eyebrows. "The Indian tribe?"

"The hotel. It's in Manhattan. They used to talk shop, booze it up. Chat a little, drink a lot, you know how it goes."

"I can relate to the drinking part," he said, in a way that was both funny and not. "Well, she sounds way more cool than Dorothy in Oz."

"I wouldn't knock either one," I said. "That Dorothy in pigtails and plaid, she had a lot of spunk."

"Yeah, I guess she did," he said. "Maybe there's something about the name."

He kept staring into me with this intensity, and all of a sudden the air in Dunkin' Donuts seemed so still, so stagnant. I wanted to be outdoors with him.

I wanted to breathe in the whole world with him.

"Let's go for a walk," I said.

JOEY

She wanted to go for a walk
get out of there.

Fine by me.

I got hit with a sugar craving suddenly so I got a jelly
donut to go. Then I shot a
quick nod to the guys at the table so fast
they didn't have no chance
to act like the dopey hyenas they are
in front of
her.

We crossed the parking lot, weaving past the cars and the
SUVs. There was all this traffic
going up and
down
the street—there's only one main road in this
pointless
town—
and so all these cars kept
barreling
by.

Inhaling all those exhaust
fumes was making me queasy. Weird, because I'd never even
noticed them
before.

Hey, Doll, I said. Then I did a
mental
face

slap.

I'm sorry, I said quickly.

She gave me that pretty smile again and I knew she
didn't care really
that I called her that.

She didn't have to say it I just knew and that was so
incredibly
awesome.

Still
I had to stop
'cause it was rude.

I said,
I mean
Dorothy ....
Wanna walk by the water?

By the water we could
breathe really
breathe in the air.

I wanted to breathe
fresh
air
with her I wanted to know how that
felt.

Like I ever gave a shit
about the air before.

Who the hell knew
why these crazy thoughts
were bouncing through my head. I just hoped they didn't
up

and

leave

as quick as they came.

      Sure,

she said. She

said,

I was thinking the

same

thing.

      We walked on the sidewalk real close

me clutching the

waxy

paper

bag

with my donut.

I was glad I had it 'cause the thought

to slip her my hand

kept popping into my stupid

brain and that was one thought that would not do.

For sure

that would be it then. You can't go doing something so bold as

that when you meet a girl not a girl like this.

But I wanted to anyway I wanted to

so

bad.

I wanted to

feel her hand in mine again

feel that energy it was like a new drug.

Hell

it was better than any drug I'd had so

thank

god

for

the

waxy

paper

bag.

> We didn't talk much on the main road 'cause the traffic
was kind of loud but it wasn't weird walking without talking like
it is with most people. With most people you're always

grabbing

for words trying to

fill in

the emptiness.

It wasn't like that with her not at all.

> We turned the corner onto a side road and
I asked her. So what did Amy say about

me?

> Oh ... nothing, she said.

> Yeah

Right, I thought.

I stopped short and

looked at her.

> Nothing ... good, she said with a laugh.

> I laughed too then.

Frigging unbelievable

that she could get me to

laugh like that.

I almost told her then
I almost told her it was true
basically
whatever Amy said
but I let it
go.
For once for
once
for
once I had a moment that was
golden
and
damned if I was gonna
ruin it by telling her what a
scumbag
I was.
     I
really
wanted to touch her
hand
and I was
so
scared
that I would
never
get to do that
again.
     Not
that I deserved to anyway. Christ

I had to warn her
who the hell
she was dealing with.

We got to the water to this inlet or something I always
forget what it's called.
It's part of Reynolds Channel but it's got this separate name.
Anyway we got to this bench by the
water
and
we
sat.

It was really warm for February even there by the
water chalk it up to global warming
I
guess.
I kind of wished there was a
cold
breeze
that way maybe we'd have to
move closer.
Still
it was something being by the
water
with her
breathing
in all that
fresh
air.
I felt high and I didn't smoke since that morning.

We didn't say
nothing
for a while we just
sat and
looked at the sun the way it
shined in
patches over the
ripples and the ducks the way they
glided over the
patches and the
ripples so smooth and
in
a
row
and we breathed we
breathed
we
breathed.
Then finally I had to tell her. I couldn't take all that
easy
breathing
no more it wasn't right.
Doll, I said.
Shit shit ....
But she smiled again so I didn't
bother apologizing I just went on.
Dorothy, I said.
Then I stopped
'cause it's hard

to tell someone what a

piece of

shit

you are.

Someone you like at least.

      I looked

down

at the waxy bag I was holding. I un-crinkled the top

took out the donut. White powder

spilled out

all over

me I was so stupid getting a jelly donut of all things why didn't I

get a chocolate frosted but what did it matter

anyway.

      It actually helped.

      See this donut, I asked.

      Yes

she

did.

      Sugar

coated my fingers

white but it couldn't

coat

the

truth.

I brought the donut to my mouth

bit a hunk

exposed

the thick globbed

purple center.

   This donut

is

me,

I told her through my

chalky

powdered lips.

   She laughed, What?

   No

really,

I said.

   I told

her,

I'm a smeary

gooey oozing

jelly

donut.

   I'm a mess on the outside, I said

holding up my free

mutilated

hand.

   And I'm more of a mess on the inside, I said

holding up the

donut.

   She said,

So?

   So,

I said.

   I

said,

So

I don't want you getting your hands

dirty.

     That's why they invented

napkins,

she

said.

     She

said,

If you're trying to tell me that what Amy said is

true

without even

knowing

what

she

said

I really don't care.

     She said, I

don't

care

about what you've done because

I see who you are

and

I know you had to

have

your

reasons.

     But,

I
said.
    But ...,
she
said.
    She
said,
But
even
if you didn't
I guess I still don't care.
Not enough to walk
away.
    Then she did it again. Oh my
god oh
my
god
oh my god
she
took
my
hand.
The one without the donut in it.
    She
said,
I've never felt
anything
like this before.
Have you?

                    I shook
my head
no.
                    We sat
quiet
for a minute
my fucked-up hand in her soft one
just
feeling that
feeling just
sucking
it
in absorbing it to our
cores.
                    She
said,
So really
the only question is
Why do you keep calling me Doll? It's a little cliched
nes
pa?
                    Nes pa? I repeated.
                    She spelled it,
N'est-ce
pas. She
said, It's French. She
said,
It means
loosely

Wouldn't

you

agree?

I said I guessed I would agree but it was just that she

reminded me of my

mom's

porcelain

dolls how they were so fragile and

pure.

I told her all this

even though I knew how un-frigging-believably gay it sounded.

Then I promised I would

stop calling her that

really I would.

It's okay, she

said.

She was still

holding

my

hand and her hair and her eyes were all shimmery

with

light

and I felt like I was one of them

ducks

out

there sailing smooth through the

water all lined up

in

a

row.

She
said,
Now that you've
explained it I
understand.

You
do? I asked. I wasn't even
sure that
I
understood. Maybe she could
explain me to
me.
Wouldn't
that
be something.

I
do, she said.
And I think it's
nice. I'm
flattered.

Go figure. I never
flattered
anyone before.
Flattened,
but
not flattered.

Squeezing
squeezing

squeezing into my
palm
she said,
And
don't
worry
I won't break.

Three

DOROTHY

"Do you cry?" I asked him.

I felt his hurt, under the charge we were sharing. It moved at a lower current, almost slipping below the radar, but I felt his pain.

I couldn't help him. I could hold him, hold space for him, but I couldn't save him. He had to find his own way through.

He stared into me, blinked like he was trying to process the question. His eyes were like the sky when the rain ends, caught between gloom and sun.

He rubbed his thumb across my skin, traced the raised artery going down my wrist. It felt coarse, like sandpaper, and it was so, so satisfying. It was like having a perpetual itch scratched, finally.

"No," he said. He drew in a breath, breathed it out slow. "No, I don't cry."

We looked at each other some more. He wanted to confess all his sins, I sensed, but I wasn't ready to hear them yet. I just wanted to know him in that moment, it was all I could take, this was all so new to me. He got that. It's amazing what you can comprehend without speaking or hearing a word if you just allow yourself. He understood it, and he respected it.

He still had that jelly donut in his other hand. He realized it just as I did—we both glanced at the donut, and laughed. He held it up to my lips. I sunk in, took a bite from the sticky center.

I wanted to kiss him then, I wanted to share the sugar on my lips, have it melt in both our mouths.

I wanted to know what he tasted like.

I wanted to know so, so much, and I felt like I'd burst if I didn't act, but I didn't.

I didn't, because it wasn't time yet.

"You need to get going?" he asked, and I did. It was getting dark, and my mom was going to worry about me. It was getting chilly, too. I shivered, wished I could fold myself into his arms to get warm.

But it wasn't time for that, either.

He wolfed down the remains of his donut, licked his fingers, wiped them dry on his jeans. Then he ran his hand up and down my arms, one and then the other, smoothing down the raised hairs. Who would ever think something so hard and calloused could be so soothing?

His other hand was still locked in mine. Neither of us wanted to be the one to let go.

I took another look at the water, at the reeds growing at the edges. So vulnerable, so exposed out there, and yet they endured.

He said, "Where do you live? I'll walk you home."

We held hands all the way to my house, about ten blocks. I

was still trying to get used to suburbia, all those houses so similar and still. Except for the occasional kids playing in the street—and there weren't many because it was dinner-time—the neighborhood was silent. You could never walk a noiseless block in Manhattan.

We didn't speak, and yet we were communicating. Getting to know each other, without words. When you think about it, words don't count for much anyway. It's the intentions behind them that count. And this was like we were skipping past the words, like we didn't need them.

"This is it," I told him when we got to my house, a Spanish-style villa, gated and set back from the road and the other houses.

He stared at the gate's crisscrossed wrought iron strips. "You live here?"

"Yeah, why?"

"Nothing … it's just … this is like, the nicest house around here. Hell, it's a friggin' mansion."

I looked at the sidewalk, didn't say anything.

"Hey, I didn't mean … it's just …. Oh, Doll." He sighed, let my hand slip from his. "We're so different."

"That's only a problem if you make it one," I said, looking back up at him.

"Yeah, you say that now …."

I took his hand back in mine. "See you in school tomorrow?"

"Uh, no … I go to Boces. That's for technical training."

"I know what it is. Okay, then come over after school."

"Come here, inside?"

I nodded. "Come over tomorrow, and you can tell me anything you want. Okay?"

"But, your parents …."

"My parents will like you because I like you. Don't worry."

His eyes looked panicked. He sucked in a burst of air, let it out slowly like he'd done earlier. The stress faded from his face.

He smiled his little side smile. "Okay."

We let go of our hands together this time, stood there for a moment, silently saying goodbye. Then he turned, ambled down the street.

He stopped at the corner street sign and gave a wave.

I waved back and unlatched the gate.

JOEY

All the way home it was a battle.

There was this new part of me

still back at the water

still holding Doll's hand.

Breathing

breathing

breathing in that air.

Feeling like one of them ducks all neat all in order all

right.

Yeah

all right.

I'd actually felt all right there.

But then there was my

other part.

The part I'm used to. The part that don't let me have nothing

'cept drinks and some bud. The part that don't let me rest for a

goddamn minute.

The part always

poking

poking

poking at my back

reminding me what a

loser

I am.

That part it don't wanna let me breathe for nothing.

That part that

part that

part keeps me frozen on the scrawny-ass ledge from the second I
wake up.

That part was saying,
She lives in a palace she's got
gates and stone pillars she's got ivy growing up those pillars she's
got all these pine trees in her yard it's like a forest in there
through
them
gates.

That
part
said, There ain't no place for someone like you behind them iron
gates.
Them gates
they were made for locking
people like you
out.
Them gates are there to keep Doll
safe
from
you.

Yeah.

It's like Pop says.
He says people like
me
if we make it past twenty
we wind up with steel bars of our own. There just ain't no
mansions behind them.

It's us that's behind them locked up nice and

snug.

      Actually, I'm ahead of schedule. Call me precocious.

      I already got a little taste of the future,

courtesy

of

Pop.

      I get the picture in my

head

so fast

before I can even tell myself

not

to go

there.

Don't matter.

This memory ain't

nothing compared to

some.

      There we are in

court.

      Again.

      'Cept this time it's not family court.

This

time on account of my

age and the

severity

of my

crime

this time this

time

this time

I made the major league. The criminal courthouse in Mineola.

    The routine in courthouses is everyone stands 'round the halls and waiting rooms making deals and whatnot to save the court's time.

    That's what we always did before but

not

this

time.

    This time they keep me

separate.

    This time they haul my ass down the hall in cuffs like I'm

some

big

shot

criminal. There's no one else around. Get this: they cleared the area first. Apparently I'm some

maniac

they gotta protect the world from.

    Suddenly I'm the bogeyman.

    They lead me right through

no

man's

hall

my hands are pulled behind my back

steel's snapped 'round my wrists.

I'm so used to the position it's kind of comforting. I got my fingers linked together it's like I'm

holding

my own hand.

      The two court officers they walk me one on each arm into
some

puke

green conference room then they

uncuff me and I sit in a

hard metal chair by a rectangle metal table just what I needed

more steel.

      In follows Mom and my

lawyer

chairs scrape back

they

sit

at the table where I

am. They sit

by

me but they don't

face

me. Mom I guess she's ashamed

of me

of her.

My lawyer

who the hell knows what his

problem

is. He's sitting there all smug in his camel hair coat or some

shit

too good for his client I guess. Then

Pop

marches in all stiff and coply like a pole's up his butt he comes in
he stands next to the flag.
I look past him out the window but all I can see from my poor
angle is
gray
sky
and the top of this sad tree its gnarly twiggy branches are all
naked. Old Mother Nature that bitch she stripped its leaves right
off
it.
      The Assistant DA rolls in he's this
puny
guy trying to be
big
in a navy pinstripe suit. He
thunks
his broad briefcase
down on the table
click
click
unsnaps it open
hauls out my record.
I got a sheet of priors that just keeps on
giving. There's
fights there's drunk and
disorderly there's smoking
bud on school
grounds and wait
there's

more.

It's all petty b.s. I never hurt no one that bad at least

up

'til

now.

      I didn't even mean to hurt no one

this

time

not like this

not to put the dude in no coma.

He just got in

my face

he wouldn't go away. Who told that

prick

to get in my face

like

that?

      Pop's

standing tall

by the stars and stripes

he's in his

neat

blue

uniform

shiny badge attached. He don't look at me

neither

not that I want him to.

Suddenly the sun casts through the window look at that it

broke

through the gray
it lands a ray right at his
black
patent
shoes. He looks like he's standing in a
path
of
light ain't that some ironic shit.
   The ADA he don't even glance my
way
no one even
turns
in my direction do I even
need
to be here? That ADA he says he's gonna let me off with
probation.
   Again.
   He don't say so but I
know it's on account of
Pop
being a cop. It's always on account of
Pop
being a cop.
But this time this
time
this time
Pop
says,
No.

We stare at him. He's standing all
righteous
arms crossed next to the
red
white
and blue. He says,
No.
He says,
Send him to
jail. Maybe it'll teach him a
lesson.
He
says,
Doubtful but
maybe.

   That's it then. My lawyer he don't do shit in my defense he
works for
Pop
not me I guess.

   Whatever.

   My mom she'll never say one
word
against what
Pop
wants god forbid.

   They bring me in front of the
judge
all rise
he seals my

fate and *badabing* we're
done.
      After that they
cuff
me.
      Again.
      They're taking me back to
lockup.
Who gives a rat's ass
anyway.
They ain't doing
nothing new to me.
I already got myself
all
locked
up
in my head.
      My hands
they're pressed together
I can
feel
my
pulse
beat.
      Mom's
crying.
      Now she's
crying.
      I made her

cry.

      They're taking me
away for four
months.

      Good for them.

      Pop
calls my name but I don't
answer. Then he
stops me he grabs at my arm he
pinches
hard
into me but I don't flinch.

      Pop
looks
looks
looks at me
he looks me in the eyes.
What do you know he
actually
looks
at me
no shit.

      I make myself
look
back it's the first time in I don't know
how
long
I look straight into the
ice

floating in them

sockets.

      The sun gleams on his badge. The beam reflects

it bounces

off the badge

it hits me in my pupil. I'm half-blinded but still I look I

look

I

look into him

into

that

frost some call eyes I won't look away

fuck

him.

      Pop

pinches into me.

He pinches into

his

son

that they're taking

away for four

months.

      In his best cop voice

Pop

tells me

he tells his son

that's going away for four months getting caged up like an animal

thanks to him

he says to

me

spattering specks of his

spit

on my cheeks my nose my lips they

seep in they

melt

in my mouth

he says,

People like you,

you

make

me

sick.

       They're taking me away now

really.

Mom steps up

she puts her arms

'round my neck

she pulls me

down

against

her

she gives me a

hug.

Feels nice even though I had to bash some asswipe's

skull

in to get it.

       Then

she lets go.

Her tears are on my neck
drip
dripping
down.
Don't cry for me
Ma
save those tears they're
awful
hard
to come by.
    I'm looking at her
'stead of where I'm
headed.
I stumble
I'd
fall
'cept for those two court officers
holding
me up
on either side
lucky
me.
    Yeah.
    Incarcerated at seventeen.
    Sweet.
    What's next? My life's
jam
packed
with possibility.

What loving father what
devoted
dad
wouldn't be delighted to see me
dating his
dear
darling
daughter?
    Doll. If she thought her parents were gonna be standing
inside them gates arms open wide like some kind of
sunshiny
welcoming committee
then she really was
caught
in a
fairy
tale.
    Of course that was
assuming
she wouldn't give me the boot
herself once she heard the things
I
done.

    I got home
stared at my house
my white house with the light blue trim and the
colorful flower beds and the
nice

mowed

lawn.

No palace for sure but

not

so

bad.

It looked okay

it looked like everyone

else's. You would never guess what went on

inside.

Maybe I could

pass

like my house. Maybe I could

pass myself off as something

okay

something normal.

      But that

prick

part of me just wouldn't shut up. It said, Who do you think you

can

fool

when you

can't

even

fool

yourself?

      Then that

new

part that poor dumb schlub who only wanted to be alone with

Doll

at the water and

breathe

that's all he asked for it wasn't much just to

breathe and be

all right…

That part piped up. It said,

Fight

for your place.

Fight for your

place

with

her.

But old part that

bastard

it wasn't finished with me

yet. It had the

last

word it always did and the worst part was it was

right. How the hell do you fight the

truth?

It said, There ain't no

place

for you and her

you stupid shit. Where you gonna

go? You'll never

pass

behind them gates and you

can't
bring
her
here.
       No.
       That was for sure. I could not bring her
home.
       She looks like one of Mom's dolls and
Pop
don't like them dolls at all
not
one
bit.

       I went inside
closed the screen door behind me so it didn't
bang.
I called out
hi
to Mom in the kitchen. She called back
hi
without coming
out.
       Too busy cooking them
potatoes.
       Every day
she makes goddamn
potatoes
to go with dinner.

Mashed
scalloped
crinkle-cut ....
      Same kind of crap
every
day.
      No one was in the living room. I headed upstairs creaking
every step. You can
never get up those stairs quiet no matter how hard you try and
sometimes
you
try
real
hard.
      At the top of the stairs is the
closet.
The closet with the ivory door and the iron gray handle and the
lock that only
Pop
has the key to.
      I hate that motherfucking closet.
      But it's just another thing 'round here you gotta face
every
single
day.
      I headed past it
down the hall
into my room to wait for
dinner.

*

Late late late
it's late.
I wake in the black
to the racket
in the air reaching up up
up from
under
me.
Pop's cursing like a madman
downstairs
high on whiskey no doubt
pacing
like a caged panther I'm
sure
he's screeching he's howling I'll bet he's
barking through the window at the
moon.
He crashes
glass
he smashes
ceramic
he bashes
Mom too I know.
My clock glares red from my night stand it's 1:56
a.
m.
My mouth tastes sour.
I lean over the edge of my bed grope for the

neck

of my Bacardi 151. I keep it tucked under the bed for nights like

this and they're pretty much

all

nights like this.

I had some after dinner but obviously I

should've

had

more.

      I nab it

unscrew

press its cool mouth to mine.

      I swallow quick but not quick

enough it's too

late.

I can't stop

them I can't stop the

memories it's too

late it's too

late I can't stop myself

I'm

going

back.

      I'm in the closet.

Seven

years old.

It's dark oh

god it's so

dark in here it's so hard to

breathe mashed against all these coats
sweaters
Pop's uniforms wrapped in
plastic
the smell of moth balls makes me
dizzy
it makes me
sick.
I'm crying coughing choking on
snot I'm trying to
breathe I'm
begging
Please please
please
Pop
let
me
out.
His fists pound the
door loud
hard they're gonna
bash through the wood they're gonna
nail
me for sure.
His whiskey breath
snakes
through the cracks.
I lean
back back

back into clothes Pop's
cold gold buttons
pressing into my
cheek
thank god there's plastic or my
tears might get on his
uniform and
what
if
they stained?
       I pee myself. I can't
help it it's warm first so
wet and warm but then it's
cold.
It wets my underwear and pants but I don't get it on the floor.
Pop
says, Shut the fuck up or I'll give it to you good. Pop
says, Better get comfortable.
Pop
says, Next time mind your own goddamn business instead of
running up all mommy
mommy
don't hurt my mommy.
Pop
says, Forget about saving no one but your own sorry ass.
Pop
says, I'm doing you a favor teaching you this
now. The key
clicks

in the lock.
   I
drop
from the work of all that
fear and crying and breathing in that moth ball air I
curl on the hard
floor with a gift box left
from Christmas for a pillow and a
cold
wet
leg.
   Later
I don't know how
much
later
   the key
clicks
again it wakes me
up. That's it just that
sound. No talking no
twisting
the handle
no one opens the
door there's just a
click
and then more
nothing.
   I'm so cold I'm
shaking my stomach's

twisting my head

hurts so

so

bad

but I can't leave not with all that

nothing

out there

not with all that

quiet

to

face.

        I lay here on the closet floor huddling tight against

myself

head bent into a

box

eyes squeezed shut

dizzy I'm so

dizzy and

sick maybe this is how a moth feels when it

breathes those

pukey

balls. I'm so

cold so

sticky I'm

shaking shaking

shaking

but I'm afraid to use a sweater without

asking.

So I lie here with my eyes shut

tight I make a game in my head to block the

hurt

hammering

away inside

hopscotch I play

hopscotch I just keep throwing down the

stick and hopping hopping

hopping

yellow number to

number box to

yellow

box I keep landing throwing hopping landing throwing

hopping hopping

hopping

in this game of hopscotch that don't

end

and I lie here I

shake I

wait.

      Wait for noise ….

      I suck down more rum try to lose the

shiver

creeping up my

back.

      Ten years later it's like I'm

still

waiting

there in the dark in all that

dead

air still cowering like a wuss still playing

hopscotch

in my head.

      I still smell the moth balls I taste my tears and snot I feel

the plastic-covered

sleeve

of

Pop's

shirt

brushing against my skin.

      I still hear all that quiet and I'm still so

cold.

      I'm still waiting for permission to come out and

breathe

normal again to

come

back

into the

light.

      Or maybe

not.

      Maybe I been staying in that

closet 'cause the dark gets

comfortable

when you get

used

to it. In the dark you know things

can't get

worse

so you can

finally

rest some.

      Maybe

it's the light I been afraid of that it might

beam

straight

down on me just melt me

down

to

nothing.

      Not that I was much to begin with.

      But tonight

ten years after I peed myself in that closet and

started waiting

tonight something's happening.

      I hear a noise.

      Reeking of the Bacardi 151 I'm soaking my

soul

in

I finally hear a voice at the

closet

door.

      It's

Doll.

She's calling my name.

      I remember how

pretty she was by the

water the way the light
sparkled
in her hair and
lit
up
her
eyes.
      I remember how
right
I felt with her like one of them
ducks
bobbing across a sunbeam all
along in a row.
      God I never thought I could swim in the
sun.
      Maybe there
is
a place for me and Doll
out there in the
open.
In the clean open
air with the sun beaming on the water
reflecting
onto
us.
      Maybe it's time to
face
the
light

again.

      And maybe just

maybe

I won't

melt.

PART TWO
THE YELLOW BRICK ROAD

"The next morning the sun was behind a cloud, but they started on, as if they were quite sure which way they were going.

'If we walk far enough,' said Dorothy, 'I am sure we shall sometime come to someplace.'"

—From *The Wonderful Wizard of Oz* by L. Frank Baum

Four

DOROTHY

"So how's everything going with Joey?" Mom asks as she stands with her spatula, waiting for bubbling pancakes on the griddle to thicken. She's using her light "shrink" voice but still there's this edge in the question, this strain in her tone. She flips too soon, and batter splatters.

Dad faces me from across the blue-checkered tablecloth. Head resting in his hands, smile pasted on his face, he's shrinking me out too as he waits for my answer. His hazel eyes stare wide from behind his wire-framed glasses.

I look away, away from them both, from my psychologist parents who are now practicing their craft on me. I survey Mom's teapot collection on the wall, glazed clay renditions of citruses and berries, plus a smattering of select vegetables and flowers. I examine a strawberry with handle and spout, note the attention to detail. There's even brown specks freckling the crimson surface, representing tiny hairs.

I regard a piece of ceramic fruit and wonder how this happened, how it came to be that I'm not comfortable in a room with my mom and dad, that the air in our kitchen feels as tense as an exam room during SATs.

I don't know what to say to these two clinicians who until about a month ago were the parents I could say anything to.

Until Joey came over.

It started with his hands. Mom got weird immediately, when she shook his hand. That's when her voice took on that soft, sing-song tone, like she uses on her patients. It was like she was trying to shrink Joey out, but even worse, because she wasn't doing it to help him. No, she was gathering history like he was in a study. You know, one of those hopeless cases therapists deconstruct, picking them apart so they can help others avoid the same fate.

Then Dad came home, and he barely spoke to Joey. He just watched him.

It reminded me of the reptile room at the zoo. Like Joey was this creature, this lizard behind glass, and Dad was observing him from the other side.

There we were in the living room, separated by the black Art Deco coffee table topped with this week's flower arrangement, lilacs. Their heady, too-sweet scent was everywhere. Mom sang questions and Dad observed from the stiff, mocha-colored leather couch while Joey sat sunken into the burgundy, overstuffed sofa across from them, hands tucked under the seat of his jeans, Nikes shuffling on the Persian rug. I sat next to Joey—cross-legged— getting more and more incensed by the change in my formerly liberal parents. Apparently an open mind closes real fast when your sixteen-year-old daughter's involved.

In her soothing voice Mom asked how old he was (seventeen), did he plan to go to college (he did not), then what did he plan on doing with his life (he was studying auto mechanics at Boces). She asked what his father did (police officer), oh, my, how did he feel about his dad having such a dangerous job (he didn't feel anything about it, it was just a job), what did his mother do (homemaker), where did they live (on the other side of town), did he have brothers and sisters (two brothers, sixteen and nine). And, of course, she asked what had happened to his hands (he sucked in some air at this one, let it out, and then said he's had some trouble with people egging him into fights). He answered Mom's questions and took in Dad's scrutinizing stare without complaint while I seethed. What was next? Maybe Mom would request blood and urine samples. Finally I said Joey and I were going to hang out in my room, and you would've thought I'd said we were going to go screw or something the way they balked. For a second I thought they were going to say no—well, at least Mom, as Dad had apparently forgotten how to speak—and if that happened, that would've been it ....

But that didn't happen, so I can't say what I would've done or said.

Mom and Dad looked at each other, like they were having a wordless discussion, and then Mom sang-songed that it was fine. She said she'd call me for dinner. Then she asked if Joey would be staying, but her voice changed. The way she asked that, like the words were phlegm in her throat that she had to hack out, of course he declined the invitation.

So much for the sing-song.

Upstairs, Joey said to cut them some slack. He said he could only imagine what was going through their heads, me bringing someone like him home, and he was only grateful they let him stay.

That made me angrier, that he felt beneath them like that. They had no right, to judge him.

And speaking of judging, they needed to trust my judgment. To trust what I saw in Joey ....

Ever since that day, it's like Dad's had this permanent case of laryngitis around me. Either that or he's morphing into an owl, the way he blinks, blinks, blinks with those questioning eyes. Like he's waiting for me to pour my heart out, explain what was going on inside that made his good little girl go so wrong.

He doesn't say it, obviously, and neither does Mom— no, she's too wrapped up in her little fake la la land voice— but I know that's how they both feel. That I've gone astray or something. For god's sake, this isn't the Victorian age. Where's my corset? Where's my chastity belt?

Mom, she's been shrinking me out ever since with that maddening tone. I have no idea how that tactic could possibly be successful with her patients but I sure wish I could cancel my appointments at the kitchen table.

And the ironic thing is, I'd love to talk to them.

I'd love to tell them how things have been, to get their advice on everything that's been happening, good and bad. It's all been so new, so much ....

First, there was that day. Up in my room. There was everything he told me, everything that poured out of him like I'd opened up a valve.

He stood in the doorway for a while, taking in my room— all my belongings, transplanted from Manhattan. Checking out my desk at the window, facing the water. It's topped with my computer, books, and inspirational quotes in frames, my favorite being Emily Dickinson's "Dwell in possibility …." Turning toward my storage hutches lining the right wall, filled with baskets stuffed with stuff, everything from more books to DVDs to magazines to souvenirs from vacations with my parents. Looking up at my vintage iron chandelier with five individual lavender shades covering the bulbs, and strands of beads draped over the arms. Looking down at the chenille rainbow-striped rug. Across at the full-length antique iron mirror, next to my dresser. Finally his gaze landed on my vintage iron bed, white with a weathered finish. It's surrounded with deep purple silk curtains on a cable system, and covered with fringe tassel bedding and a red, pink and violet calypso floral quilt and sham. It looks like Bohemian meets preppy, which kind of describes me. Joey headed to the bed, picked up my obese stuffed orangutan and gave him a squeeze. "That's Ollie," I told him.

Joey plopped Ollie back among the pillows and chuckled. Then he traced his fingers around one of the two throw pillows monogrammed in green with "DJF," for Dorothy Jane Fields.

"You got your initials on your pillows?" he asked.

"And my bathrobe," I said.

He laughed. "Is that is case you forget who you are?"

That made me laugh. "I guess so. I never thought about why I had them before."

He walked back around my curtain, brushing against silk and stirring something inside me. He eyed the white trunk at the foot of the bed. "What's in here?"

Amazing on how he zeroed in on my most private, embarrassing possession. "That's my hope chest," I told him. I smiled at his raised eyebrows. "It's not like those chests girls put things in for when they get married. I put my hopes, my real hopes, in there. I put in pictures from magazines of things I aspire to and places I'd like to see. I put in poems expressing feelings I hope to feel, books I hope to memorize passages from and carry in my heart, articles from the newspaper about things I'd like to change in the world and ways I can make a difference; and I write down things I hope for—wishes and dreams."

"Wow," he said. He bent down and batted the chest's brass handles, banging them on the wood. "Pretty big. Holds a lot of hope, huh."

"Yeah, I guess." I was guessing a lot, all of a sudden.

He smiled that little smile of his, with an added twist of wistful. "Maybe you could, like, share some with me sometime." His eyes were big and bright with that plea again, like in Dunkin' Donuts. Like something inside was desperate to break through, break free. "I could use some hope."

"Sure," I told him. "We can open up the chest anytime you want. Or even better, I'll help you find hope that's all your own."

He studied me for a second, his gaze steadier now. "Good luck," he said.

We sat on my bed, staying at the corner and keeping our feet on the rug just in case one of my parents popped in. First we talked about them for a bit—as I said, he totally defended them. Then he asked, was it okay to tell me now? Could he tell me about himself? And to tell you the truth, I would've loved to not know because he looked so sad about it all it had to be bad, but he was determined to get it all out and I knew it would stay between us until he did. And anyway, I'd promised him that he could.

He took my hand and it was so exquisite feeling that sensation again. It was so exalting it was almost torture, because I knew I'd have to eventually let go. And he looked me in the eyes—he looked at me with all his pain, and I held his stare even though it made me want to cry—and he went through each thing he'd done, starting with schoolyard fights in which no one had been seriously hurt, escalating to when he'd beaten another boy so bad he'd been in a coma for three days. He said that was when he'd been sent to jail. He said he didn't know why he'd done that, the only explanation he could offer was that he walks around on the edge. That's how he put it, that he teeters on the edge constantly and sometimes people just push him over.

God, he looked so sad. I should've been horrified, probably, but all I could think about was how sad he looked. He'd been so concerned about damaging me, yet he was the one who seemed broken.

He was telling me these stories about how he'd hurt people and the more violence he confessed, the more bound I was to him. It was his honesty.

He was exposing his soul to me.

I couldn't possibly turn him away.

He told me he drinks and smokes weed. He said he wasn't going to lie and say he'd quit, because he wouldn't. He said he wasn't proud of himself doing these things, and he'd try to cut down, but he couldn't give them up completely because they were sometimes the only things that got him through.

Got him through what, I asked.

He stared at me for a few beats, wordless. It was like he was running something through his head—or maybe, he was running away from it. Finally he answered, "You know, through life. In general."

But I sensed it was something way more specific.

Back in the kitchen, Dad blinks, blinks.

Mom flips at the griddle.

I lean back in my chair, think back to what happened two weeks later.

Joey and I were hanging out with a big group of kids at the spot they go to drink. It's this little bridge connecting two parts of Highland Park divided by water. They like it because if the cops come by, they can pitch their bottles right over the side. Mom and Dad would've died if they knew I was there, but I wasn't doing anything except talking. I just wanted to be where Joey was, get to know his crowd.

I have to say, they seemed to have more depth than Amy. At least while they were coherent.

I was talking to a couple of girls in denim jackets about song lyrics in heavy metal, and how intense they could be. I told them about the poems of Robert Frost and Robert Browning, and how profound I found them. But as the girls got more and more wasted on beer their attention and eye contact drifted, and finally they wandered away. Then I got hit with the sickening sweet scent of weed—god, I hoped I didn't stink of it when I got home. It smelled kind of like the lilac bouquet in the living room, though, and for a second I thought maybe Mom and Dad wouldn't know the difference.

Yeah, right.

I moved away, slid down the bridge railing a bit, craning for Joey. There were at least three dozen people there now, and he'd melted into the throng. Everyone was stoned and laughing, the mix of voices getting louder and louder as the six packs and liquor bottles emptied. I leaned against the metal, stared out into the dark waters, at the boats roped at their docks, bobbing faintly with the current. Up, down, up, down. They made me feel lonely, and I wished I could just go home.

"You okay?" A male voice behind me asked.

I turned around, faced him—a boy in a black T-shirt and jeans. He had a lanky build and sand-brown hair. "Where's Joey? You're ... with him, aren't you?" he asked.

I nodded. "He's in there somewhere," I said, motioning to the burgeoning crowd.

"I'm Brian," he said. "You're Dorothy, right?"

I nodded again. His breath was hard to take. Vodka, I'd guess. I knew what most alcohol smelled like on people, from my parents' parties.

"So, you named after Dorothy in *The Wizard of Oz*?" Brian asked. His words wobbled.

"No." I'd answered the question about a dozen times that evening, and I was too tired to elaborate.

"Oh," he said. There was a pause as he tried to think of what to say next. Inebriation runs contrary to intelligent conversation.

I leaned back against the railing, sighed. Brian found something to say, but I wasn't listening. I stared at the moon in the distance above him, round and shimmering, beaming lines of light into the tide. Looking to the side of Brian, who slurred on, I watched a lone duck float through a moonbeam.

"What the hell you doin', man?" Joey's angry voice yanked

me back to the bridge. Joey was leaning into Brian, poking his finger into his chest.

"Nothing," Brian said, moving backward. Joey moved with him, practically on him. "I wasn't doin' nothing, I swear."

"I seen you over here, talking to Doll." Joey's voice was even more sloshed than Brian's, and he reeked of that horrendous Bacardi 151.

"Who's Doll?" Brian asked.

"Don't act like you don't know who I mean." Joey gave Brian a shove. "Dorothy. She's with *me*."

"Joey, stop," I said. I couldn't fathom these caveman antics. "He was *talking* to me. So what?" I grabbed at his arm. He shrugged me off, bunched up the front of Brian's shirt into his fists. Brian had backed up as far as he could. The steel railing pressed into his lower back from behind, while from the front Joey pressed his weight into him.

"Shit, man," Brian sputtered. "I'm sorry, all right?"

"No, it ain't all right," Joey barked at him. "It sure as shit ain't all right." Despite those angry words, he let go of Brian's shirt. I thought he was done, that he'd come to his senses. Instead, he clasped into Brian's neck, hanging Brian halfway over the railing and throttling him.

"Oh my god! Stop, Joey," I screamed. "You're killing him!" Brian was bright red, gurgling and convulsing. The whole crowd semi-circled around us, watching, but no one did anything to help. "Joey, look at me. I'm begging you …." He ignored me, continued to choke Brian, who flailed helplessly. "*Joey, look at me.*"

He did it then.

He let his fingers slip looser, turned my way. His eyes were glossy, wild with rage. I didn't know this Joey.

"Let go of him," I said quietly. "Please."

He looked back at Brian then, with surprise, like he didn't know how he'd gotten there, on top of this guy he was strangling.

He let go.

He moved off of Brian, who sank coughing to the walkway. The crowd moved in then, surrounding Brian, offering him drinks and assistance. Now, they cared.

He came over to me, tried to touch me. I moved away. "Don't," I said.

He looked at me again, then, his eyes still glossy but now tame—remorseful. "Doll … I'm sorry. I don't know why …."

"Joey, you almost killed him."

"No … yeah, I know. I don't know what happened to me …."

"Gee, maybe that rum you were guzzling happened to you." I started walking. I should've done it earlier.

God.

Someone had almost died.

Because of me.

He followed me through the streets, all the way home. "Doll, Doll, come back. I'm sorry," he kept repeating. His voice tapered, getting lower and lower until it dropped off completely, leaving him silent behind me except for the sound of his scuffling sneakers and his labored breathing.

At least he kept his distance.

At least he didn't try to touch me again.

Halfway down my driveway I turned and saw him there.

Illuminated in streetlight, peering through my gate, hands gripping the bars. Lost. Forsaken. I almost gave in, went back to him. But then I thought of those hands clenching Brian's neck. I thought of Brian's veins bulging between those fingers, trying to flow.

I shivered, went inside.

For a week he called my cell phone over and over, leaving apologetic, pleading messages.

I finally picked up. I'm not sure why. Maybe those things they say about time are true. Or maybe I just missed him more than I hated what he'd done.

He'd never do that again, he swore. He'd stop drinking the rum. I was right, it was the rum for sure, he agreed. He said for now on, he'd only drink beer.

For him, that was something.

I forgave him.

That night, right before I went to sleep, I opened up my hope chest, slipped in a paper. It read, "I wish Joey would stop drinking."

But even as I closed my trunk, I knew he wouldn't. I knew he wouldn't because of what he'd said, about the drinking and smoking weed getting him through. I knew there was something eating away at him, gnawing bit by bit at his soul.

I just didn't know what it was.

The smell of pancakes wafts through our kitchen as Mom stacks them up. Dad blink, blinks at me. I stare away, at an orange teapot, complete with little pockmarks all over it, just like a real orange. Whoever made it must've pecked away at the orange with a mini-spear or something.

You have to give those teapot sculptors credit.

They're good.

I drift back to a third memory. Last Saturday, two weeks after the incident on the bridge. Joey and I had seen each other every day since I'd forgiven him, but it had taken me a while to feel comfortable letting him touch me. He respected me, he tried nothing. He was just happy to be with me. Finally, on Thursday I let him hold my hand again. I slipped it to him while we were walking back to my house, and it was there again—that magic. It was like nothing had happened, nothing had changed between us. That made me relax completely, and I asked if he'd like to take the train into Manhattan on Saturday. He said sure, although his enthusiasm dampened when I suggested we go to the Met—the Metropolitan Museum of Art, I explained to him. Apparently he was not a huge art connoisseur. Still, we went.

It turned out that Joey had never been to a museum, except in the first grade, when he went on a class trip to the dinosaur rooms at the Museum of Natural History. That blew my mind. I'd lived most of my life just a few blocks from the Met, and had gone there almost weekly. So I took him around, showed him the Egyptian exhibit and tomb, and the medieval section with all the thick suits of armor. He was amazed; he hadn't even known these things existed anywhere, least of all thirty miles from home.

Then I took him upstairs, to the paintings.

To my favorite place in the museum, and possibly in the world.

To the Monet room, a place where you could actually be among some of the finest works of Claude Monet, who was in my opinion the greatest of the Impressionist painters. Monet was infatuated with gardens and water and often depicted both. He created stunning pastel-colored, dream-like portraits of nature.

This room is my sanctuary.

We circled the room slowly, weaving through people, taking everything in.

The last painting was my favorite. Bursts of lavender water lilies floating on an ethereal pond. I turned to tell Joey how much I loved it, but stopped when I saw his face. I didn't have to tell him—he felt the same way. He was mesmerized, steeped in thought. It was as though he was trying to figure out how to enter the painting. Or maybe, somehow, he had.

After a while he turned to me, smiled that little smile.

"Thanks," he said.

I took his hand, led him to the bench in the center of the room. Surrounded by beauty, we sat.

We sat crooked, his denim-covered knees touching mine in grey tights. I felt this tingling through my legs and I inched closer into him, into his arms.

God, I felt so safe in those arms.

So, so safe.

Then he kissed me.

There were all these people milling around the exhibit and then just like that there weren't. They evaporated, they melted into the air. It was just us, then. Just us left, and the water.

Us in the water, kissing softly.

He held me tight, like he was my vessel guiding me across.

I melted then, too, but not all of me. Just the hardness,

the coating over my everyday life. I didn't need its security, because I had Joey. It vaporized—poof!—and I was free to be me.

I realized then, as I reveled in my freedom, that the covering I'd been sheathed in hadn't been shelter, not anymore. It had started that way, but it became a pall, obscuring me. A facade—a camouflage of who I was supposed to be, but wasn't. It was the personification of everyone's expectations.

Everyone except Joey. He's the only one who didn't expect, or assume. He gave me room to breathe.

My shell had gone from protection to prison, and I hadn't even noticed. I'd been locked inside—safe, but alone. I'd spent so much time being who Mom and Dad wanted me to be that I'd never gotten to explore who I truly was. I just didn't know it until now.

In my sanctuary, kissing Joey, I knew it was safe.

Finally, it was safe to be me.

Mom's finished cooking and we're all at the table. She and Dad both blink at me now, waiting patiently like good little therapists for my answer to the question she asked ages ago, and which she's just repeated: How's everything going with Joey?

Isn't my session over yet?

This is what it's like now, at my house. This is what it's come to. Meet the shrinks. If they'd just be my parents again, I'd spill it all out.

I'd ask for help in reconciling the two Joeys. The one that's headed for prison, or worse—and the other, who set me free.

"Fine," I say. Our pancakes are in plates in front of us, losing steam. "Everything's going great. Pass the syrup, please."

JOEY

Snap.
Crackle.
Pop.
Me, Jimmy and Warren
crunch
cereal. We're playing
the
game
looking at the
sunny yellow wallpaper
looking at the white light on the
ceiling looking at the bananas and the
oranges and the red and green
apples in the bowl in the middle
of the table looking
everywhere
except
at them.
Pop's jabbing his finger at Mom,
he pokes
into her arm,
he yells she's a worthless
bitch.
My
head
feels like it's gonna
pop

right off my neck, it's gonna
burst
wide open
like a sledgehammered
watermelon—
shimmering crimson
gunk splattered
over green linoleum and
bright
sun.

   Jimmy crunches away he chews on he doesn't give a
shit let 'em kill each other that's what he thinks.
I think that's a good excuse not to help her but
what's
mine?

    But it's not my
job
to save my
mom
is it?
Aren't I the
kid?
Is it my
fault
she chooses to stay with
this
prick
she married?
Once

I asked her if she
knew
before.
I asked her if she knew what he
was
when they were
dating.
She said she didn't. She said he was just
old
school
Irish
Catholic.
She said he wanted a housewife to
cook and
clean
and she didn't wanna work anyway she wanted someone
solid
to support
her.
Yeah, he was solid alright he packs a nice
solid
punch
don't he?
I asked her why she
stays.
She said she stays for us for
me
and Jimmy and
Warren.

And for a while after that
conversation
she was my
hero
she was my
home
warrior
keeping the family
whole.
But then it came to me what a load of
shit
that was. She don't stay for
me
and my
brothers she stays for
her.
She stays 'cause it's easier than
going
than taking care of
herself and not knowing what's out there in the
cold
dark
world.
She's got no one else to count on that's for
sure.
Back when
Pop
started being
Pop

she went to her mother and tried

telling her it wasn't

working

out.

My grandmother she's not the

sympathetic

type.

She told my mom: You made your own bed,

enough

said.

       Grandma stopped visiting when I was

little after

Pop

told her to eff off one time.

But I think she was glad to be done with

us

anyway to leave us with the

mess

Mom

chose.

Grandma wasn't exactly overflowing with

warmth.

Touching her was like getting a

brain

freeze in your

body.

The really funny thing is that out of them three

Pop

is the

only
one who ever
brought
up
love.
He loves Mom he tells her
sometimes
when he's not
hitting
her
and I think he means it too.
But Mom I don't think she loves
Pop
not one bit.
She takes what he gives
the good the
bad
this is her
life so
be
it.
       Now Doll
comes into my head.
Me and Doll with all them paintings water
water
everywhere.
Sweet sweet Doll oh god I can taste her lips they're like oxygen
pure
oxygen a dose of fresh air

they're hope
she tastes like hope.
For the first time
I'm not hopeless.
We're kissing
I'm hoping
and the room turns slow
all them paintings swirl around us
they
take
us
in.
We're gliding through them lily pads
swimming we swim we're breathing
underwater
we blend we mix we melt right into them whirling bursts of colors
where everything's
connected where everything belongs where everything's
right.
The world's so right
finally
it all makes sense
but then
I
quit.
I quit I quit I
quit kissing her I
push
her

away I let her float back to the surface.
It ain't right
swimming with her
using her to
breathe
like that.
I can't I can't I
can't take the chance of dragging her down to the murk with me.
She don't belong at the bottom
of the pond she don't belong
here
in my kitchen.
I can't let her be
here
even just in my mind she might get muddy.

   Warren's scared he blinks blinks
blinks his
big
brown
eyes
he forces slow spoonfuls he stares at
fruit.

   Me
I'm waiting to wake up.
I been waiting to
wake
up
from this nightmare years too long now. It's getting harder and
harder to fool myself it's real tough playing

"pretend

you

don't

see."

　　　　His bacon's

sizzling

on the stove his eggs are

whisked

in a bowl

waiting

to be poured on the

griddle his coffee is drip

drip

dripping

its last drops

into the pot his orange juice is

freshly

squeezed with

pulp

strained.

　　　　His face is beet-colored he's all up in her face she's backed

against the counter

nowhere to go and it

won't

be

long

now.

　　　　I wanna wake up

in a normal family where my

pop

kisses my mom good morning and reads *Newsday* at the table,

where my

pop

never raises his voice let alone his hands, where my

pop

loves his family, where my

pop

loves me.

      For seventeen goddamn years I been waiting for my pop to

love me how stupid is

that?

      In a desperate attempt to either

escape

or

give

up

my mind floats back years and years to

another

morning.

      Me and Jimmy

playing on the living room floor with

Lincoln

Logs.

Mom's eye is purply-

blue it's half-closed. Her lip's

scabbed

blood around the

crusty

edges and
puffy it's all puffy from what
he did
last night.
> Pop tells her to make him breakfast.
> She says,
Make your own
breakfast.
> Pop
says
nothing. He's
red. His face is bright
red
like a Fireball candy. Hate's
dripping
from his skin like
sweat I can smell it.
> He lifts up the
love seat.
It's brown like the coffee she
brews for him everyday
but not
today
it looks like the coffee when she stirs in cream
it's creamy brown.
He holds the
love seat
high
he grips it tight so

tight
the veins in his hand bulge
thick
and
blue.
He slams it
bam
he
bashes the
creamy
brown
love seat
down
down
down
on Mom's back. She screams she
howls
like a dog like
an
animal
that don't know how to
mask its
pain.
She falls she
falls
she
falls
arms up like she's
surrendering

hair slapping at her
face
white apron strings flap
flap
flapping. The floor rumbles it rocks it
shakes
when she hits
bottom
bent and
broken.

      Her eyes are shut.

      Round logs
topple they
spill they
roll
they
scatter.
Some hit the wall.

      Mom quivers like she's
cold like she's freezing she
shakes. She looks whole but she's
broken.

      Her eyes are shut.

      Me and Jimmy's log house is broken like
Mom
but it's in pieces you can see.

      Her eyes are shut.

      Back then,
she still cried.

Back then,
I still
believed
really I believed
that I would
wake
up.
I truly believed I would wake up and Pop would
love
us that he would
love
me.
Pop's pounding Mom to a
pulp.
I stare at the
clear
glass
bowl on the counter at the
beaten
eggs inside.
Eggs just waiting to
run
free across the smooth
non-
stick
surface. But they can
only get so far
before they reach a raised edge.
Snap

goes Mom's shoulder.

  Crackle

goes Pop's bacon frying in the pan. The greasy smell is everywhere.

  Pop

goes

Pop. He pops Mom

again

again

again.

  Pop.

  Pop.

  Pop.

Five

DOROTHY

I ask him, "Was it awful, being in jail?"

Joey's silent, he's holding me against him, stroking my hair. A few seconds go by, then he says, "Well, I wouldn't file it under 'fun.'"

We're in his friend Jason's garage, converted into a workout room. Jason's mom works a second job nights, and his dad left town long ago for parts unknown, so the guys come here to weight train and to hang out without being hassled. But on days when no one is working out, Jason lets us come here for some "alone" time. I told Joey we could go to my room after school since my parents are at work until at least 5:30, but he said no way. He said he has a strict moral code when it comes to parents and their homes. He even admitted that it doesn't make sense, but he won't touch me under my parents' roof. I think it's strange, that he draws a line there, but it's kind of nice, too. And it's just as well. I could never really relax in my room. There's no lock on my door. Every little sound would freak me out.

Not that we've done anything, really. Just make out. We've been making out a lot. And holding each other. We're doing that now, lying together on blue exercise mats piled on the concrete floor, with a thick black punching bag turned sideways behind us. You couldn't really call it a cushion, because that implies soft, and this bag is hard. This bag is no pillow. This bag was made for endurance, not comfort. Still, you take what you can get, and you do the best with it you can. It bolsters us, supports us.

My head's tucked in the crook of his shoulder. I nuzzle against his shirt, breathe the scent of him. Spicy sugar. He's mulled cider by the fire on a snowy winter day.

His heart's beating, *tha-thump, tha-thump.* I say, "I'm sorry you went through that."

He says, "No reason for you to be sorry—you didn't send me there." *Tha-thump. Tha-thump.* "Besides, I deserved it." He sounds so hollow again, he sounds haunted. I keep thinking, if I can only figure out what's at the base of all his misery, then I can help him release it. That's why I'm bringing up jail. Because maybe that's what's tearing away at his spirit—those lonely, scary hours he spent in jail. All I want is to exorcize those ghosts, fill in that gap inside.

"That was mean of your dad ... to send you there."

Tha-thump. Tha-thump. Then a sigh. "Pop's not the nicest of guys."

"I'd say not."

"Listen, Doll. Could we drop this? I just ... I just wanna be alone with you. I don't wanna bring Pop in here, let him lie down with us, okay?"

It's the same thing, every time. No matter where we are. "Okay," I say.

He strokes me some more, so gentle. His leg's wrapped around mine, so warm. "Thanks."

We're surrounded by workout equipment here in Jason's makeshift gym. Some is Jason's, but more belongs to guys who have no place of their own to set it up. Three bench presses, leg machines, arm machines, and lots of barbells in different sizes. The radio propped on a bench in the corner is playing an eighties tune, "I Melt With You." The singer declares he'll stop the world. It feels like that here—now and whenever we're here—it feels like the world's stopped. He touches me so slow, so tranquilly. Hard to believe hands roughed up like that could feel so soothing. Harder even to reconcile those tame hands with the devastation they've caused.

They're so respectful to me.

They're practically reverent.

He kisses like that too. With this sweet serenity, like there's only us. Like there's no such thing as time.

He does that now, he kisses me. He pulls me closer against him, presses tight against me, and that tingling rises again, from somewhere way inside me. It's always there, always going, always generating when I'm with him, but when he kisses me like that, that's when it escalates. That's when it demands attention.

He feels it, I know. It's what hit us when we first met, times a thousand.

He feels it, but he never acts on it. I keep waiting for him to move further, to act. But he doesn't.

And I ….

I don't know how to.

Only this time, I can't take it.

I slide my hand under his T-shirt, glide across ribs and ripped muscle. His body jerks from the sensation. Heat surfaces, melts into my touch. Slow, slow, I smooth my fingertips up the middle line of his chest, tracing the indentation. He pulls back. "Stop, you're making me crazy."

"Is that a bad thing?" I ask.

He regards me, looks at me like I'm some new creature he's discovered. I stare back into those wide eyes, waiting for an answer, acutely aware of the blood push, push, pushing through my veins, and wanting only to brush his skin again.

Still, he doesn't answer.

I say, "It's been three months. Do you not want to make love with me?"

He jolts at the question. After a few seconds he finds his voice. It's rocky. "You kidding?"

"Then why …."

I leave the words dangling, reach for him. I pull his shirt up, up, over his head, then slip it from his arms.

He doesn't resist.

I lean against him, press my fingers into snug chest fuzz.

I don't know much, but I know I want him.

"Why …," I say again, and again that's all I say.

I push my chest into his, reach my hand behind, drift down, down, down the small of his back, until I'm tucked inside his jeans.

His heart rate quickens, drums its beat into me.

Thump thump thump thump thump thump ….

I rest my lips against his ear, share the shiver they provoke. "Why don't you?" I ask.

JOEY

The question zaps through me like ten thousand volts.

Why don't

I

make love with

her?

Because I never held

anything

so precious before.

Because I'm afraid so afraid ....

I tell her,

I'm afraid I'm gonna break you.

She laughs. Says, I'm not a doll silly.

Silly. No one's ever called me that before.

Dickwad.

Scumbag.

Piece of shit loser.

Not silly.

I like it.

It's light.

I wish I was light.

With her

with

Doll

I feel like I got a shot at being light.

What are you thinking, she asks. She's touching

touching

touching me.

I'm thinking
I don't wanna ruin it ruin this.
Ruin
her.
I'm thinking I'm gonna hurt her
somehow
I'm thinking I'm scared for her
and maybe even of her.
But I don't tell her that stuff 'cause it'd make her bolt for sure. You
can't show fear
you can't show
yourself
even if you feel safe enough. Safety is bullshit. There is no safety.
More things I can't tell I could fill a book with them.
She's waiting for an answer
I know
but I'm not saying nothing I'm like a deaf-mute or something.
Why she's bothering with me I don't know. I don't deserve her I
don't deserve her touching
touching
touching me like this and god I'm so afraid I'm gonna hurt her.
I never done it before, I tell her.
I tell her I never made love.
She looks at me now she's got this skeptical look she don't
believe me.
It's true,
I tell her.
It's true I never made love never did it with no one I cared 'bout
before.

I had sex I screwed but I
never
made
love.

     She's touching
touching
I lie here skin prickling temperature smoldering arms frozen so
scared to touch back so scared I'll become
the monster Pop is;
the monster
I am
when I lose it lose
control.

     My first time,
I tell her,
my first time I was fifteen it was August it was hot so hot
me and Jimmy we were at my cousin Billy's pool chilling.
Billy he was twenty and he had a bunch of friends over too. This
chick Libby she was nineteen she had these great round tits they
were practically popping out of her hot pink bikini she started
rapping to me then she sat on my lap next thing you know she
was tonguing me.

     That night
me and Jimmy we banged her in room twenty-four at the
Beachview Motor Inn.

     She blew me at the pay phone on the street while I called
my mom to tell her me and Jimmy we was
eating
out.

It was like that every time since. Not the situation but the
emotion.

There wasn't no emotion.

Just going through motions.

I feel something trembling.

It's

me.

How can I touch her like that touch her pure
pure skin? My hands they're so mangled they're ruined like me
beyond repair I'm bad so bad she's pure she's good and

I'm

so

bad.

She kisses me she's undeterred by my tale of debauchery
she kisses me her soft
soft lips against mine their moisture sinks inside me she quenches
my thirst.

She kisses me and I get it. Suddenly

I get it

she don't care what I done she don't care what I

am

she takes me

shit and all.

Like someone opened a window

I get it

a blast of fresh air

I get it I kiss her back and then just like that

I

melt.

It happens so fast I can't scream or despair

can't panic

can't blink

I just melt.

No regrets no goodbyes I melt through her arms I melt to the mat

then

I

rise.

I rise without burdens

no voices

in my head

there's light

silent

light

lifting through.

No worries no doubts

only light

calm still light

I feel something light

it's me.

      It's me

and Doll

in the quiet

alone and I'm light I'm

light I'm

light.

      Touch me Joey, she says.

      She says, Please.

      So I do.

DOROTHY

His eyes fill with light, so beautiful. I watch the pain melt from them. Drip, drip, drip, it shrinks down, it just shrivels away 'til it's gone. They're happy now.

He's happy.

I made him happy.

JOEY

She's letting it all out it's like there was all this shit stuffed way inside her that she finally gets to let out.

I'm letting it out.

For once I'm doing something good.

I'm following her now I'm scrambling up a mountain sprinting up up up scuffling over rocks darting around trees splashing through streams there's a place for us after all there's a place for us it's here at the top of this mountain it's where we can lift off we can leap we can sweep through the sky …

oh god

I'm flying

the breeze on my face it feels so incredible

I head for the clouds

I'm right behind her now

I catch up I take her hand.

Six

DOROTHY

"Happy birthday, Joey," I tell him. We're in Jason's garage once again. We get to use it about twice a week. The rest of the days we make out by the water, which is pretty great too. I've suggested hanging out at Joey's house, but he won't go for it, and he won't say why. He just changes the subject. It's been nearly four months and I've never even seen the inside of his house, or met his parents. Of course we could go to my house—it's not like my parents barred him, but they sure wouldn't make him feel at home, either. Things haven't improved in that area, but the good news is there hasn't been any noise pollution emitting from the Fields residence.

So, it's the water for us when we can't borrow the garage. I don't know what'll happen in the winter, but we'll tackle that when it comes.

I cuddle close against him, press my skin into his. His pulse is tranquil now, it's come down from its heightened state. "Want your presents?"

"You mean there's more?"

"This wasn't a gift, we do this all the time."

"This's everything I want," he says, and I know he means it, but he's still getting his stuff.

I hoist myself up, grab his crumpled Black Sabbath T-shirt, throw it on—I like to wear his shirts because they're long on me and they smell like him—and I head to the corner where I hid his presents under a bench press. "Jason let me drop these off yesterday," I explain, carrying three gifts over to him, two small and one large. They're wrapped in firecracker red paper, which in fact does have lit, sizzling firecrackers depicted all over it, together with the words, "Hope your birthday's dynamite!" Corny, but colorful. I plop them in front of him on the mat. He sits up, pulls them in. He's still naked, and all those muscles in motion look so luscious, I have to do a mental slap so I don't jump his bones again. Not that he would mind, but I do want to see how he likes his gifts.

He takes the card from the top, slips it from its envelope. It has a quote from Emerson: "What lies behind us and what lies before us are small matters compared to what lies within us." He reads it, laughs. "You are so friggin' deep," he says. "The guys, if they'd buy one at all, they'd pick out a card about farts or something."

"A fart card was my second choice," I say.

He opens the card, reads what I wrote. It says, "Joey, I hope this year brings you as much happiness as you give me. XOXO, Doll."

"Gee …," he says. He pauses, swallows hard—so deep that his Adam's apple swerves, it oscillates in his throat. His mood veers also, I can feel it. It takes this dip, this plunge, like the mere mention of happiness sends him plummeting.

Damn.

But then he snaps back, he fights his way up again, and he smiles. "Thanks," he says. I smile back, but it sucks, it really sucks, that everything has to be a fight for him. Every little thing, inside and out.

I want to take him in my arms, hold him, but I don't.

Not this time.

I can't shelter him from himself.

Paper crinkles, tears as he opens the first gift, one of the small ones. It's a book, my favorite book. He lets the wrap drop, holds the book gingerly, tentatively, like some foreign object—perhaps something that might ignite in his hands. "*The Catcher in The Rye?*"

"You've never read it?" I ask.

He shakes his head no, leafs through pages.

"Holden Caulfield reminds me of you," I tell him.

"Yeah?" He scans the beginning, raises his eyebrows. He flips to the middle, reads a little more, and arches those brows even higher. He asks, "In what way does this dude remind you of me?"

I don't want to tell him now, on his birthday.

I don't want to say I think he and Holden are both running from something, searching for something, that they're both lost and lonely. Because as much as Joey's with me, here with me, he's also not.

He's missing—a part of him is missing. It's severed from him, out there somewhere all alone.

"In ... in a metaphysical kind of way, I guess," I say.

"Oh." He laughs. "That explains it."

He puts the book down and opens the next gift—the larger one. *Rippp! Rippp!*

Out of the shreds he raises the lid of the box, takes out one of the blue boxing gloves I bought him. He holds it, regards it with a look I can't quite discern. I say, "Since you like to fight so much, I thought maybe you could, like, put your ability to some use." He's wearing such a bizarro, incomprehensible expression, I wonder if I've treaded too close to his space somehow—if I've violated his perimeter. Who am I to tell him he should box?

But then he nods, shakes his head. "Yeah," he says. He smoothes his hand over the cool leather surface, smiles that little smile that melts me every time.

He slides his hand inside, flexes. "Yeah," he repeats softly, and the word sounds comfortable.

It suits him; it's right.

It fits him like the glove.

JOEY

   I
squeeze
my fingers inside the glove.
   Feels snug it's
warm.
   It's like settling into cushions on a thick cozy couch it's a
place to lay my hand and
rest. A
refuge a
padding
from all the knocks my hand gets self-inflicted though they may
be.
   So I guess it's
protection
from
me.
   Now that's funny.

DOROTHY

He sits for a while resting his gloved hand on his lap, on his bare thigh. He's quiet. It's almost like he's meditating. I let him be.

After a bit he smiles again, and he says, "Thanks, Doll."

"You're welcome," I say. "But there's more." I raise the third gift, the other small one. I dangle it in from of him, trying to entice.

He tugs the glove off, puts it down next to him. He accepts the gift, unwraps. His finger slits into the tape this time. The paper makes a wrinkling sound as he unfolds it.

What looks like two rolls of surgical bandage in black fall into his lap. "Wraps," I say, in case he doesn't know. He gives me a brief 'duh' look before turning to what he's holding, the other thing that was inside the paper—a gift certificate for ten boxing lessons at the local muscle gym, Iron Land. "Jesus," he says, staring at the words. "This had to run you some real bucks."

I shrug. "You're worth it."

He says, "I could never …."

I touch his arm, sink my fingers against his skin. "Don't do this," I say. "Don't turn this into something ugly. I don't care what you can afford to get me, just like you didn't need or expect any gifts. Just enjoy it, Joey, okay? That's your gift back to me, if you enjoy this."

Our familiar electricity tingles between us, and he relaxes. "Okay," he says.

"So, you want me to wrap you up?"

"You know how?"

"Sure. George—that's the boxing instructor—showed me when I took my lesson."

"*You* took a boxing lesson? Why?"

"What's the matter, afraid I'll kick your ass?" We both laugh. Then I say, "I wanted … I wanted to know what it was like to punch things."

"You like it?"

"Uh, no."

He chuckles. He knew darn well I wouldn't. "Why not?"

"Well, for starters, it felt very confining in those gloves, and they never seemed like they were on right. It was just about impossible to get a grip in them. And it hurt to punch! George said I was hitting with the wrong part of my hand, but I just couldn't get it. Then there was that speed bag. Talk about humbling, I felt like a complete spazoid trying to hit it. George said I'd get better with practice, but there are some things you know you're just not cut out for. And anyway, it was just too much work, all those moves—too much to concentrate on. Yeesh."

"That's a relief," he says. I unravel one of the wraps, and direct him to reach his arm out straight, spread his fingers wide. I smooth the wrap around, around, loop it around in tiers, coating his hand and wrist so it's taut but not tight. He says, ""For a minute I was afraid you were gonna leave me to headline in Vegas."

"I'll leave the championship fighting to you, Rocky."

JOEY

She's like a nurse treating her patient she's
bandaging my
wounds. That's how it feels like she's
blanketing my hand—my
motley mutilated
poor
excuse
for a hand.
She winds it she
winds
it she lays it
on me
over me she
covers me in
tender
layers.
Safe
I feel safe. Comforted. It's like when I wore the cuffs
when I held my own hand.
It's like wearing the cuffs without the
cold
steel without the
shackling.
Who knew who
knew who
knew
I could feel good

without
feeling
bad.
All those nights
I spent in my bed hands huddled under my belly clutching at my
fingers trying to find something
some
way
to feel better caught in that trap in that hell under siege overrun
by all that screaming thrashing
bashing
going down
downstairs
all those nights these wraps they would've been perfect.
Powerful I feel
power like I'm jam-packed with power
energized
I feel
control
heated sweeping control Jesus Christ for the first time I feel
control.
Fuckin' A.
I don't never wanna take these mothers off.

DOROTHY

He's so peaceful now, he's got this calm easy feeling to him. He's still got the wraps on, he's naked except for the wraps, he's holding me with the wraps on and I feel like I'm with a Cinderella man, like these wraps are the equivalent of a dress for the ball, trimmings for a new life.

He leans his head on mine, his pulse beats into my crown.

"What are you guys doing later?" I ask. He's hanging out with his friends tonight, and unfortunately that pretty much guarantees the consumption of alcohol. I worry about Joey—he hasn't gotten into any really bad incidents since the one at the bridge, but he's had some scuffles. I always feel like he's one drink away from disaster. Still, he's so tranquil now, so level. It's hard to imagine him hurting anyone, but it's like he said — for him, there is no sanity, no normal. He could snap at any moment. He also said when he's drunk, he starts to think that's the real him — that's who he truly is.

And that is one frightening thought.

"We're gonna play cards."

Super. "You mean you're going to play drinking card games," I say. Those games have such enticing names, like Circle of Death and Brain Damage.

"Yeah, I guess," he says. "You can come, if you want."

He knows I won't. "Thanks, but I really don't feel like watching you destroy your liver in endless hands of Drink Bitch."

"Are you a teenager or, like, a parent?" he asks. His tone is kidding, but he's half-not.

"I'm someone who's confident enough to know I don't have to drink to have fun."

"Well, excuse me …," he says. He takes in a breath like he's about to say more, but he doesn't.

I don't want to argue with him. It's the last thing I want, especially today. And I also know that for him, the drinking isn't just about partying, getting stupid.

If only it were.

His pulse is still thumping into my head. I close my eyes, try to get lost in the rhythm of it. But I have to ask…

"Joey … you're only drinking beer, right?"

He says nothing. There's only the *thump, thump, thump.* Faster now.

I open my eyes, face the concrete wall ahead of us, face the black poster hanging. The Nike symbol's on it, in red. The words 'Just Do It' are printed in stark white underneath. "Joey …."

"C'mon, Doll. The guys'll think I'm a wuss if I don't drink the rum."

"Oh sure, you can't have them thinking you're a big pussy," I say sharply. I pull away now, turn and face him. "Afraid they'll think you're whipped?"

He doesn't answer. He looks torn, like he doesn't want to fight either, but also like doesn't want to give in, change his intentions.

That stops me.

He doesn't want to change.

If he doesn't want to change, what am I doing here?

Deep down, I've had this plan. That I'd find out what was

eating him, help him confront it, and poof he'd be okay. He'd stop drinking and smoking weed. He'd change.

I assumed he'd change.

But what if he doesn't? Even when I get through to his core, what if he doesn't want to change?

What if the real Joey *is* the drunk Joey?

Oh god.

JOEY

That Nike poster hangs in front of us it's like a red cape
flagging a bull.
Just do it.
Just
do
it.

Yeah right.

How many times can I just do it before I wind up back
behind steel bars or buried
in a wood box?
Asshole
I'm such a thick shithead.
Doll all she wants me to do is
think.
Think.
Think before I
just do
it.

Here I am giving her grief and that's all she wants.

DOROTHY

I'm staring off somewhere. I'm not even looking at him. Then I hear him say, "Okay."

Cotton rests on each of my cheeks, his fingers touch my temple. He's staring into me, bringing me back.

Back to him.

His eyes are earnest. "Okay, you're right. I promise, I'll just drink beer tonight."

As ludicrous as that affirmation is—he really needs a ride to AA for his birthday—I feel intense relief. He's not slipping away. He's on the level field with me, he's playing my game.

I can still hope ....

I can still believe that one day he'll stop drinking altogether.

One day, he'll stop. He'll change.

He wants to.

He kisses me, and we fall to the mat together.

DOROTHY

It's 9:11 p.m. and I'm channel surfing on the couch with Mom and Dad. I was supposed to go study with Amy and a few other girls, but I wasn't in the mood. I've decided that Amy's okay if you accept her as she is—her primary goal in life is to be popular and admired, but hey, you have to appreciate that she's up front about it. And once I made it clear that I was going to date Joey no matter what anyone thought, she accepted it. I don't like all the gossiping, though, and so I can only hang out with her and her crowd now and then. And tonight, I didn't feel up to it. I just want to veg, after all that went on with Joey. It was beautiful, but it was exhausting.

He had to go home for dinner, he said his mom always bakes a cake for him on his birthday. I wanted to go with him. I wanted to meet his family; I wanted to sing to him; I wanted to watch him wish and blow out his candles. But he wouldn't let me come. He wouldn't even discuss it. At first it seemed like he was going to say something, tell me something. He had this anxious air around him, like he wanted to spill something out. Like in my room that day, when he told me everything he'd done.

Was there more?

But then he pursed his lips together and swallowed—it was as though he choked down the words, forced them down his throat—and when he did speak, his voice was firm. He said, "Doll, trust me. You don't even wanna go there."

It was good that I came home, anyway. My parents both made an attempt to talk to me at dinner—Mom's voice was actually normal for once—and over spinach fettuccine, salad, and garlic bread we had a lively conversation about school and about their new offices in Garden City. That's why we moved, because they brought their practices to Long Island. They got a great deal in a luxury building, saved a bundle in rent, and now they have adjacent suites and lunch every day. Cute, isn't it? Anyway, I was so happy to have parents back that I agreed to hang with them afterward, watch tv.

I'm sandwiched between them, and it's nice. It's like old times.

Dad's flicking through channels—we just caught the tail-end of *Good Will Hunting*. Huge faces flash by on the giant plasma screen as Dad now hunts for something we'd all enjoy. There's the *Law and Order* guys, there's Jack Nicholson trying to hack up his family in *The Shining*, there's Queen Latifah in one of those feel-good-about-yourself-no-matter-what movies, and now there's the Lollipop Guild, welcoming Dorothy to Munchkinland.

Dad leaves it on.

I say, "You know, those Munchkins really make me laugh. Dorothy kept telling them she wasn't a witch, but they just wouldn't listen."

Mom says, "Small-minded."

Dad says, "You think that's the real point of this movie?"

I say, "Let's not psychoanalyze *The Wizard of Oz*."

JOEY

This whining little motherfucker Holden Caulfield
what's his
problem?
If I got packed off to some
candy-ass
boarding school if they shipped me the fuck outta
this
place I sure as hell wouldn't do nothing to get booted out to get
sent
back
home.

I'm laying in bed reading this book just 'cause Doll gave it
to me I wanna know what the hell she thinks I have in common
with this
tool
who trolls around
sponging
for company and
cocktails.

Cocktails.
Christ.
Drink from the bottle dude.

Meanwhile I bailed on my friends tonight. I was just too
tired after all that stuff with Doll god what an awesome day and
then I came home I had
cake with Mom Jimmy Warren and
Pop.

Pop
actually gave me a
rap
on the shoulder wished me
happy birthday
but in a way that's harder when he's
cool
it knocks me
off my
game
when I get a taste of the
Pop
the rest of the world knows. The
stand
up
guy who'll always pull over to help someone
stuck on the side of the
road. Mister good time who's
cracking his buddies up
so amusing
down at the bar
plus
he's buying the next
round.
No one knows the
Pop
behind our
closed front
door.

So anyway I was just too frigging exhausted and I wanted to lay
down and read my book.

      I got my wraps on now
I put them on again.
When I got home
before dinner
I came right
upstairs
brought up all my stuff to
my room and I
unraveled
my wraps.
I did it partly cause I didn't feel like explaining or
sharing yet with no one about the
boxing
and also on account of I wanted to
keep
them
clean.
But I looped them on again as soon as I got in my room
after cake.

      Doll did them better so
neat so
sleek so
perfect like a
new
skin
how'd she do that? Now they're
lumpy they're

thick they're

bulky clumps I look like a

mental

patient fresh from a suicide try gone wrong but who gives a shit

my hands they feel amazing.

      I think of her again I think of Doll I look over at the card

she gave me it's

propped

up on my night stand next to a

half-empty bottle of Bud.

I promised I wouldn't drink no rum so here I am

downing

piss-warm

beer

aww it don't matter anyhow

it does the same job in the long run.

      I think of

her

the way she wanted to

come over tonight she wanted to

meet

my

folks yeah that'd be something.

I wanted to tell her I almost did I almost let it all loose about

Pop.

      The words were there at the

edge

of my tongue they were ready to

leap

but I
stopped
them I stopped them I
stopped
them I gulped a wad of spit and shoved them words
down
down
way the hell
down 'cause I'm
scared.
      I'm
scared
she'll leave me that
that'll
be
it
my freak show family is too much for her
I'm too much of a
freak
for her.
      I'm
scared
to tell what my
pop
is how he hurts my mom how I
watch.
      I'm
scared
she'll think I'll

be
that monster one day and I'm
scared
she'll be right.

I'm scared of changing the way she sees things
forever
changing the
shading
of her world
she's got no
clue
how
dark
things can get.

I been
covering
so long I'm
scared
of the light. Even after today after all we been
through
even though I felt so
light
with her still I can't do it I can't show myself
in
this
light it's too much.

Me and my family
we been passing so long.
People

pass

us by

they

pass

our house our neat flower beds our

shiny

aluminum siding

all those

stupid

smiling

people

all those

deaf dumb blind

dense like a brick passers-by

they got no idea

what's

up

inside.

What would they do if they knew?

      She wants to come in.

      I'm scared.

For me.

For her.

      I can't tell her.

      Ole Frank Sinatra he starts wailing away downstairs on

Pop's

stereo.

      Come fly with me.

      It's a signal to me

it's like the Bat Signal reversed
'stead of telling me to
spring
into
action it's telling me to stay put in my cave.

      It's a signal that
Pop's
getting hammered he's slamming them down getting ready for
another night of hammering.

      Something crashes sounds like glass.

      Sinatra wants to
pack
up and fly
away.
Not an option,
Frankie
baby.
Not yet.

      I fold my arms
together.

      Tight.

      Soft black cloth
coats
my goose bumps it
settles
those little raised hairs.

      Happy frigging birthday to me.

      Cheers.

DOROTHY

We watch the Wicked Witch of the West sink to the floor, shrieking all the way.

I ask, "Why on earth would anyone keep a bucket of water around when they know it could destroy them?"

Mom says, "It's just a story, honey. You can't think about it too much."

Dad says, "The bucket has to be there. How else would they melt the witch?"

My point exactly.

Seven

JOEY

     I must be
nuts
bringing her here when I swore to myself
I
wouldn't.
But she kept at me
she wouldn't let up she wanted to meet my folks she wanted to see
my
house she wanted to see my
room.

     Yesterday my mom got a call she found out my grandma
in Florida came down with double pneumonia. So Mom she took
Warren they flew down to go see her and they won't be back for
three days.
Doll
when she heard that
she got this idea to cut
out of school come over my house while
Pop's
working his shift.

We didn't get to borrow Jason's garage
at all this week on account of him and some of the
other guys
training
heavy
for a lifting contest
so that left us
outside and horny.
       Even if I
broke my
word
to
myself
and agreed to go to her house when her
parents
are working, we couldn't. Her mom
finally found a housekeeper she liked
enough
to hire for
keeps
she was testing them out since they moved here.
Guess she's as picky for her
home as she is for her daughter.
Hey you can't blame her.
So I thought,
Why not bring her
home?
We get some inside
alone

time and it'll make her
happy she gets
part
of what she wants.
Maybe that'll be enough.
    Christ I hope so.
    I gotta admit it's unbelievable having her here in my room
in my bed she smells so good she's like a Glade Air Freshener in
my stale world maybe her scent'll linger when she's gone.
    We're laying here holding each other
just finished making love
we did it the minute we got through my
bedroom door
we just about fell onto the bed in a
tangle.
She wanted to do it downstairs when we walked in she was all
over
me I was about to lay her down on the couch but then I caught
that old
love seat
in the corner of my
eye
and then I just
couldn't.
    I didn't tell her that of course add that to my list of things
I don't
tell her
makes me feel so bad but I
can't.

I said, Slow

down

okay? I said, Let me show you the place

and

then

we can hang out

upstairs.

       I

watched

her walk through the living room

the dining room

into

the

kitchen.

Part of me it thought, Maybe she'll

guess. Maybe she'll

sense

the truth

now that

she's

here.

       I couldn't pinpoint if I wanted that to happen or not.

       The good news is the

inside of my house

passes

just like the front

apparently

'cause she passed through every spot where Mom gets

beaten

like nothing.
Even in the
kitchen
she couldn't tell she stood right by the stove she stood right where
Mom
stirs
those potatoes and
eats
lead
and she
didn't
feel
nothing.
She didn't get
jumped
by that feeling of doom it grabs me it sinks in my chest it wraps
round
my
heart and twists
twists
twists
when I
step
on that linoleum she didn't breathe in that fear
the whole kitchen
reeks
of
it's built up like grease on the walls she didn't hear
my

mom's

cries

they vibrate through my bones

even though she stopped crying so goddamn long ago.

      I don't know if I'm

thankful or

betrayed but

this time

she didn't

feel

my

pain.

      She said it's so

nice she said it's so

homey.

She said

my house it's so neat

and practically

immaculate.

She was

surprised she'd thought maybe there'd be clutter

chaos

a heaping mess

maybe that's why I didn't want her there.

You could say that,

I

thought.

You could definitely say that.

      She said she'd had visions of

filth she
laughed she
said
the way I acted trying to
keep
her
away
she was expecting
maybe even
pestilence.
   Yeah.
That's it exactly,
I wanted
to tell her.
I wanted to
shake
her I wanted to
scream, We're
surrounded by filth and
pestilence don't you
see it?
   Poor Doll she thinks my house is clean but it couldn't be
any dirtier.
   It's
stained
there's streaks everywhere they don't never come out no matter
how much
you
scrub.

After that
after we left the kitchen
I felt off I felt
woozy maybe even dazed a little
like when a bird
smacks
into glass
and then lies there all stunned
it was kind of like that.
I staggered away
at least in my head
I guess I seemed like my regular self 'cause Doll she
didn't
notice.
       We headed
up
to my room. When we got to the top of the stairs I
hurried her
past that
closet.
If we lingered
there if I got caught in that
trap
then I might've spilled it all out
I might've messed up everything
the mood
our plans
her
I would've spoiled them all

by telling her
the truth by dragging her into the
dark
with me.
      Once I got her through my
door
it was okay I felt
okay
again I let out my
breath
I didn't know I was holding it in.
I felt all the
good
stuff she makes me
feel I felt all the good flowing from her
into
me.
      And all that other
stuff that
bad
stuff
it just lifted up up up off of me.
She was kissing
kissing
kissing me she was touching me I could breathe again and it was
okay.

DOROTHY

His room's the color of midnight.

Some would call it black but they'd be wrong.

It's darkest blue, it's got the slightest dab of white in it, barely noticeable but undeniably there.

I wonder if that tinge of white mixed in midnight is dawn. I wonder if dawn's there always, inside the night. I wonder if dawn's tucked somewhere in midnight's folds, safely stowed until its time to shine.

He holds me close, and I can feel the warmth. I feel the light inside him, spirited and hopeful.

Waiting.

Waiting for its time.

His room's the color of him.

We're cuddling on top of his comforter, which is black. His bed's centered against the back wall, facing the door. Other than his night stand next to us, his dresser to our left and his bike parked to our right, his room's pretty stark. Even the floor's bare wood.

The few personal items in sight are from me. His boxing gloves and wraps are on top of his dresser—he actually wears the wraps most days, if we're not going to get completely physical. My birthday card is on his night stand, along with *The Catcher in the Rye*, which he's almost done reading even though he says he can't stand Holden Caulfield. He does have posters on the walls: Ozzy right behind us, eyes crazed and mouth baying; AC/DC, Nirvana, and other bands scattered around the room; and on the ceiling above the bed there's some model in a bra and panties.

He apologized for that, but I couldn't care less except that it's sad for her to have to put herself out there like that, with her body twisted into a seductive pose which is ridiculously unnatural.

"Kind of a let-down, isn't it?" he asks, breaking into the quiet. We haven't been able to share complete silence for over a week. It's a great thing to be so comfortable with someone that you don't need to fill up every moment with words.

"What is?" I know he doesn't mean the sex.

He strokes my arm. "My room."

"Why would you say that?"

He sighs. "It's just … it's just, nothing really." His fingers smooth, smooth over my skin slowly. "It's pretty empty."

"Well, it may not have many furnishings," I say, "but any room with you in it is far from empty."

He smiles, kisses me.

A few licks later I add, "And, it's our first time in an actual bed."

"That it is." The mattress frame squeaks as he pulls me on top of him, and that's the end of conversation.

JOEY

We're climbing
climbing
heading up that
mountain
when suddenly
she
jerks
her body
jerks
back
she screams in horror now in
pain
her body jerks back
and she's
off me she's
gone and I see
him
he's got her by the
hair he
yanked her right
off
me by her hair it's
Pop
holy fucking god it's
Pop.

DOROTHY

god
oh my god what's
happening who is this
man?
he's a cop he's got a blue uniform a badge
he's
got
a
gun
oh
god he's gonna kill us

JOEY

She's hysterical she don't know what's happening to her I wanna help her save her but I'm frozen I'm fucking useless staring at his gun in its holster. Could I grab it before him? I don't even try I'm such a piece of crap wimp.

Don't hurt her

Pop

please let her go, I beg him but I know I

know

he don't give a rat's ass how much I beg matter of fact he probably feeds off of it.

Who's this little cunt? he booms.

Pop

Please ..., I say. I wanna jump up jump

him

but no I just stay there

stuck.

And no condom

either

you stupid shit, he yells.

I say, I'll do anything you want

Pop

you can do whatever you want to me beat me whip me you can rip my goddamn head off just

please

let her go.

Pop

laughs. How

sweet, he says.

He says, All worried about your
girlfriend?

Should've warned her what could happen when you brought her
home.

DOROTHY

He called him
Pop
Joey called him
Pop
oh my god it's his
dad
this monster is his
dad.

JOEY

He looks
down
at her she's
quivering
kneeling naked on the cold floor his hand's gripped round a
clump
of her hair she's crying
quiet
now I could kill him.

How old are you, he asks her but of course she don't
answer her eyes are shut and puffy and those tears they're still
pouring
pouring
her face it's like a waterfall. He yanks on her hair she just
whimpers it's like she don't have the
strength
to scream anymore.

Sixteen she's sixteen leave her alone
Pop
please, I beg him. I don't think he'll do nothing crazy to her he'll
get caught
she'll tell she ain't Mom but then
who
knows
what's in his mind.

Statutory rape, he tells me.
He says, I could bring you in.

I say, Fine do it cuff me just let her get dressed let her
walk
away.
Relax I ain't gonna hurt her, he says.
He says, I'm just gonna teach her a lesson while I'm
taking
care
of
you.

DOROTHY

He's gonna
hurt
him.
Joey, I
cry
out I reach for him but his dad
pulls my hair
again he tells me to
shut
the
fuck
up.
It's
okay Dorothy, Joey says his voice is
soothing he's trying to make me feel
better he called me Dorothy not
Doll
how can he be
calm when his dad's gonna
hurt
him?
Oh god he's gonna hurt him.

JOEY

I call her Dorothy not
Doll
'cause I don't wanna make Pop think of them
dolls
and how she
looks
like
them.
I tell her it's
okay I don't know what else to do.
Pop tells her to
get up
I say let her put a shirt on for chrissakes
he tells me to toss it to her. I throw her
mine it's longer covers her
more. He lets go long enough for her to
poke her head and arms through the
holes tears and snot's smeared all over her face she's still
beautiful
though
then he grabs her arm he says, Let's
go.
Where're you taking her, I ask I start to climb off the bed
to follow but Pop says, Wait
here.
He says, She's going in the
closet.

No Pop no please not the closet, I beg she'll be so
scared in there it's
so
dark.

But he's taking her he don't give a fuck there's
nothing
I can do so I tell her, Close your eyes Dorothy
close
your
eyes and make a
game in your
head.

I tell her, Don't worry 'bout me I'll be fine just
close your eyes
play a game it'll be
okay.

DOROTHY

He
shoves me
in
I
fall against plastic covered clothes they
swoosh he says keep
quiet or it'll be worse on my
boyfriend does he even
think of him as his
son
god he's gonna hurt him.
The door
slams
shut the key
clicks it's so
dark so
tight in here and Joey's
out
there
with a
madman.
What if he
snaps and kills him what if he
kills
us
both?
A scream wells in my

throat but I

choke

it

back feels like I'm suffocating on

phlegm and the smell of

mothballs. I

sink

I curl on the

floor I

stretch Joey's shirt over my

knees slide my arms

inside the sleeves I

cocoon

myself.

I clamp my eyes squeeze

them squeeze

them Joey said

keep

them

shut Joey said play a game so

I

do.

      I think of a

jump

rope I'm in the middle of a

jump

rope it swings itself round round

round it

slaps

the ground it

whips

around I

jump

jump jump oh god I'm so

scared I

force myself I jump I

jump

I

jump.

JOEY

He comes back in just as I get my jeans buttoned he's got
that
steel
look he always has for
Mom.
He hates me he hates us
all and I don't even know
why.
I wanna ask again for him to
let
her
go but I don't 'cause I know it's
useless he thrives on this shit
hurting
us its like what two
double
AAs
mean to the Energizer Bunny he can go on and
on and
on ....
He takes out his gun I guess he means to
scare me but he
don't I'm too far
gone to care all I care 'bout is
her.
Her white blouse it's crumpled up next to my pillow I
reach for it I

touch

it

it's something of her to hold onto.

He smashes steel against my face feels like I'm torn
open feels like my teeth are
knocked clean out I check for them with my tongue they're still
all in
place I'm bleeding but I don't
care.

He presses the muzzle of his Glock against my neck it's
cold it's
chilling shivers run through me down my spine.

He clicks the safety off. He ain't gonna shoot
me that much
I know.
He might beat the crap outta me but he ain't gonna shoot wish I
could tell that to the little
raised
hairs on the back of my neck he ain't gonna
shoot
me and I ain't gonna
cry.

Fuck him.

Maybe that's why Mom stopped crying. Maybe she's
giving him the big
F you
when she takes it all so calm. All this time I thought she was
giving in but maybe she's telling him to
fuck off

wouldn't that be something.

So I'm doing okay 'til I think of Dorothy again all
alone
in that closet and then I gotta fight
hard for the first time in I don't know when I
fight
off
the
tears.

He always said he didn't wanna see no
tears he always warned
us not to
cry but I think now maybe he was
glad when we did it because it meant we were completely
down
pinned to the mat.

He looks at me his eyes are
solid blocks of ice motionless and
frozen.

He's a cobra he's coiled and ready he's always
ready to
strike.

He's cold-
blooded cold-
hearted the more he pounds on me the
calmer he gets the more his temperature
drops.

He don't smell neither somehow he don't
sweat he don't get

worked

up

at all.

      He's got those

cold

snake

eyes

their ice seeps into me it

melts into my

soul he strikes

he strikes he

strikes

striking's all he knows.

DOROTHY

I jump
jump
jump
to the beat of my
heart steady steady
steady
not too fast or I'll
fall
I squeeze
my eyes jump
jump he's hurting Joey he's
hurting Joey he's hurting
Joey
I jump I jump I
jump.

JOEY

He hits me again and I see stars it's not just an expression
that shit
really
happens.
     I'm holding onto her blouse like a
lifeline wish I could put it to my
face breathe in her
scent but I know I'm
covered
in
red I don't wanna stain it.
     He
slams
me a few more times I lose track of how many I'm slurping down
blood I wanna
pass
out I wanna
sleep I wanna be
gone so bad but I hold on for
her
I gotta be awake I gotta get her out somehow. If I give in I don't
know when I'll be back so I
hold
on.
     I guess he gets tired or bored he
stops he says there better be no next time or
else

he leaves it at that and believe me that's

enough

as I drink my blood cocktail makes me think of 'ole Holden

Caulfield where's my

straw.

My face feels like a

slab

of beef ready to serve up with

potatoes

I guess I know what a cow goes through getting pulverized do they

at least

kill

it

first?

He's walking

away he says he's gotta get back to

work he says he came by to get his

sunglasses.

I can barely move my jaw or my

puffed

up

lips but I do it

I call out to him I say,

Pop

can I have the key?

He stands there I can't be sure 'cause my eyes are all

swollen but I think he's smiling.

Bastard.

I say,

Pop
please let me get her out.

   I say it again I say,
Please.

   The key it
lands on my lap it makes just the smallest thud it's like that *Horton Hears a Who!* book Mom
used to read me but I hear it 'cause there's no other noise in here
'cept for me breathing.

   He's
gone but I call out to him again I call him back.

   What, he says.

   I say,
Pop.

   I cough I swallow more blood Jesus Christ does it ever
stop coming I
clutch the closet key in my
hand the jagged ridges press in my palm I say,
Pop
if you
touch
her
again
I'll kill you.

   He laughs that motherfucking prick laughs like I said
something funny.

   He keeps on
laughing
all down the hall.

DOROTHY

Jump jump jump jump jump jump jump
jump
jump.

Eight

JOEY

He broke her.
She's sobbing she's
leaning into me
sobbing she's shaking
shaking she's
quivering
in
my
arms.

When I opened the door there she was
huddled up on the floor
tucked inside my shirt like a turtle goes in its
shell when it's scared she was
rocking kind of
swaying she wasn't
crying she was
chanting something to herself I think 'cause her mouth
moved but she wasn't saying nothing and she wouldn't
open her
eyes.

I bent down by her I said, Doll it's
me.
I touched her shoulder god that felt
so
good
touching her again but she didn't
move she didn't
flinch she didn't
stop her chanting.
I said, He's
gone.
But she wouldn't
look at me she wouldn't even
nod I wasn't sure if she
knew I was there her lips they kept
going with no sound coming out and all I could think was
he broke her.
I picked her
up from the floor I
carried her into the
hall. She was like
dead
weight
in my arms but her body heat
pulsing into my chest it felt
oh so alive.
I told her
it's
okay
now

and that's when the tears came.

   She won't open
her
eyes she's
crying she's crying she's
shivering christ what can I
do?

   I'm so sorry, I say so
useless I'm
useless I can't
help her now and I couldn't
stop
him from hurting her from
breaking
her she's
trembling
I can't stand it
he
broke
her.

   I wanna fix her I wanna make her feel
good put her
back
together oh god
he
broke
her.

   Her tears run down my shoulder my neck my
back they tingle they make me
forget my throbbing face for a second. My blood

globs in her hair I'm
ruining her
even
more now I bend my head to kiss her cheek the
salt from her tears stings it
burns.

      My blood her tears they
mix
together looks like a runny cheap salsa she's shaking
shaking she won't open her eyes what have I
done
to
her?

      I do the thing I
can do the
one thing I
know
how to do the
only thing
I'm good at.

      I touch her
touch
her touch
her she makes this
one
little startled cry and
then she
stops.

      She stops crying.
      Thank god she stops

crying her body
loosens she stops
trembling
she lets out a sigh and she
drifts
to
sleep.

      She's resting
now she's
dozing in my
arms I've got her back
in my arms I
nuzzle
her
hair I breathe breathe
breathe
her
in and then I
let
go finally I can let
go I can
rest I
follow
her
lead I
sleep.

DOROTHY

I wake up sticky so sticky coated I feel painted with
something I open my eyes I see I'm covered in his
blood.
God his face his beautiful
face it's like he's been hit by a train
he's
wrecked.
He's asleep I fight off the tears I don't want to wake him.
My head's throbbing it's so hard to think
clearly I feel
fractured
I've got to pull myself together I've got to be
strong for him for
us.

JOEY

She's awake she's watching me when I
come back
when I wake up. She's got this
pity on her face and I think, god what I must
look
like and I hate it
so much
that she has to worry 'bout me on top of everything else.
　　　　She shouldn't have to feel bad for
me
this ain't her fault.
　　　　She kisses my
hideous
swelled
lips I wince I can't help myself
it's like a bolt of pain's been shot through me and her eyes they get
all wide she apologizes and I say, Don't.
　　　　Slowly it's so hard to talk through my redesigned jaw I say,
Don't be sorry
ever
you are the one
right
thing in my life and I don't care how
much
it
hurts
I want you to kiss me.
　　　　But of course she

don't
kiss me again 'cause she just
can't
bring herself to now that
she
knows it hurts me she's the
only
person I ever met who cares like that.
        So much there's
so
much
swarming through my
head
now
way too much to say or even
understand
but she strokes my hair and I feel all her
caring and somehow
she does understand
I know she does
and she
whispers, Joey
why didn't you
tell
me?
        And out of all my reasons my
twenty
thousand reasons why I couldn't tell her the most
selfish
one pops up in my

pulsing

thrashed

mind

I think, Because you'll leave.

      And I don't wanna say it 'cause I'm so scared it's true and

I'm scared of my thoughts and I'm scared of this

whole

bullshit

world

what chance do we got but a voice inside pipes up it says I gotta

tell her

and I know it's right I been

keeping it all inside

way

too

long.

      I'm

afraid you're gonna leave me, I tell her.

      I tell her, I'm

afraid it's the

right

thing for you to do.

      She

touches me

again she runs her fingers through my hair she says all

soft, I won't leave you Joey.

      And I

believe

her I know she means it and something

bursts

inside
me and that's when I
lose it I
cry I cry I
cry.
       I can't remember the last time I
cried I
sob into her shoulder and my face it's on fire from
touching
her and from the
tears but it feels so
good
even though it feels so bad
'cause it's coming
coming
coming
it's been such a
long
time
coming.
       She
holds
me while I cry no one's
ever
done that
for me
she holds me while I
cry.

DOROTHY

He's crying.
Thank god, he's crying.

JOEY

The tears finally slow and I feel really
good for someone who just got my
face
smashed
in. I feel cleared. Like I
cleared
the
way
for me to tell her
everything.
So I spill it all out. Slow and clogged
sniffling and snuffling
throbbing
there's thumping in my head like an elephant's stomping my brain
through
all
this
I tell her 'bout how me and my brothers we watch our mom
get her ass kicked just about every day that for us it's part of the
routine like brushing our teeth. I tell her 'bout how
Pop
always said not to cry not to say nothing or we'd be
next. I tell her 'bout the
closet how I been locked in there
all
these
years in my mind I tell her 'bout

Mom's

dolls the whole truth how

Pop

hated

them and god I should never have brought her here what the hell

was I thinking?

      I tell her, You really need to go home and never never see

me again.

      And I mean it I

do.

Look at her covered in my blood and tears and snot look what

he

did

to her

to me

and the most damage it's what you

can't

see.

It's gonna be worse next time I can't protect her from him I'm

a big punk pussy all the boxing lessons in the world ain't gonna

change that they ain't gonna give me the courage to stand up to

him

next

time

he's gonna shatter her he's gonna smash us

both

to

bits.

      She looks me in the eyes.

She looks she
looks she
looks
me
in
the
eyes.
      I never seen more truth in my life than what's in her eyes
right
now
it sears into me it melts through my
shame she looks at me and
she
says, Joey we'll find our way
through
this.
      She
says,
Joey I love you.

PART THREE
THE GREAT OZ

"The four travelers walked up to the great gate of Emerald City and rang the bell. After ringing several times, it was opened by the same Guardian of the Gates they had met before.

'What! Are you back again?' he asked, in surprise.

'Do you not see us?' answered the Scarecrow.

'But I thought you had gone to visit the Wicked Witch of the West.'

'We did visit her,' said the Scarecrow.

'And she let you go again?' asked the man, in wonder.

'She could not help it, for she is melted,' explained the Scarecrow."

—From *The Wonderful Wizard of Oz* by L. Frank Baum

Nine

DOROTHY

I tell him, "I love you, Joey, and it doesn't have to be this way."

He stares at me. His energy shifts. I feel it moving, shuffling. A coolness surrounds him, hardens over his skin like a shell. He says, "And how do you know how it has to be?"

The words sting like he slapped me with them. Instinctively I turn away, face the bars on his banister across from us.

"Love." He doesn't say it, he spits it. "What's love? Shoving someone headfirst into a wall? Smashing a fist in their eye? Vowing to cherish someone forever and then cocking a goddamn gun down their throat?"

He touches my shoulder, I flinch. "Look at me," he says, and I don't want to but I do, 'cause god help me I love him and I brought this on. I look at him and I'm trying not to cry but it's no use. He says, "See my face? This is love, Doll. This is what love does." His eyes … oh god, his eyes they're cold, they're almost like his dad's right now. He says, "Love, hate, love, hate …. Can't you see how they blend?"

We stare at each other now, me crying, him causing it. If I

could, maybe I'd leave, but I can't go home like this. Then his eyes change. Just as quick as they chilled they melt, they're the warm eyes I know, and they're sad, so sad. He says slowly, "Just don't say you love me, okay?" His voice sticks on these last words, like he's holding back something. Maybe more tears, maybe something else entirely. He says softly, "There's no such thing as love, Doll." His voice is a murmur. "Love's just hate wrapped with a bow, dressed up all pretty in pink 'cause we can't take seeing the naked truth."

And I'm still crying, but not for me. For him. For the life he's had that's made him say this, believe this. Part of me wants to argue, part of me wants even to yell, but I can't expect him to go against what he's been taught his whole life.

I can't walk away, either.

I take him in my arms, hold him tight. He wants the love he doesn't believe in, so badly he wants it, his body's begging for it right now. This is where we are, this is where we're stopping for today, so be it.

"Okay," I tell him, I whisper in his ear. Then I kiss him there, on his lobe, it's the one spot untouched by his dad. "Okay, I won't say that."

He lets out a long, crazed moan and then he cries again.

He weeps into my shoulder.

JOEY

I finally stop
finally
I get myself
together she's still
here.
She's still
here she's got me in her
arms even though I'm such an
asshole.
I can't believe she's
still
here
with all that's happened
with the way I talked to her
with the mess I am
she's still here.
But she can't exactly
go home looking like
this.
Maybe she should tell her parents she should
spill it all out
at least then she'll be safe from
Pop
from me.
Me I'll go back to being dead it's what I do
best.
She deserves so much better than

this they oughta arrest me
all right not for statutory rape but for statutory
hell I brought her to
hell tossed her right in the
fire I delivered her to my
demon like a
sacrifice.
Yeah she consented to come she
pushed to come but she's too
young to know better too
innocent too
unaware
she was so goddamn unaware
look
what I did to her
look
what
I
did.

      I should say something but
what? Everything's so
jumbled so
scattered all I know is I hurt her but I
can't take back
what I said
it's all I got to
hold
onto
I can't let go or I'll head right

the
cliff.
      Without my tears I feel
hollow there's an
echo in my
soul. I wonder if there's
anything
else in me
good or
bad is anything left inside me at
all?
      Doll
she's been holding me
so
long.
I pick my head up strings of
snot stretch from my nose they
snap they fall
back on her shoulder.
I been crying on my Led Zeppelin shirt it's my
favorite. I face her and I have to say
something
anything but I just can't I'm too
tired.
Then she looks at me and just like that it's
okay.
I don't have to tell her anything she
knows.

She knows
it's all there in her face
she gets everything I'd say if only I had the
strength
she gets it all she
knows.
      She strokes my hair feels so
good like
relief after my
release
then she says she needs to go.
      She says she needs to
clean up
go home
her parents expect her for dinner. It's almost dinnertime we came
here at 9 a.m. and look at us now
me with my bashed in
face
her with her bashed in
innocence what a
difference a day makes.
      Part of me wants to rush her
out send her safely on her way but the other part the
selfish part
it wants to
keep her by me 'cause I'm so
scared.
      I'm scared to be
alone here

I'm scared to shut my
eyes tonight.
I'm scared if she leaves I'll never
see her
again
and I'm scared that's the way it
needs
to be.

      I say, Let's get you in the shower.

DOROTHY

I want Joey to leave, too. "What if he comes back?" I ask.

He shakes his head slowly, painfully. "Pop ain't coming home soon," he says. "No way he's cooking for himself, and if he's eating out no doubt he's drinking out too. He'll be out late."

"But eventually ...." I can't bear the thought of Joey alone here, a target waiting.

It's like he reads my mind. "Jimmy'll be home, probably."

"Even if he is, what's Jimmy going to do against your dad's gun..."

"He's done with me for today, Doll," he says. "I'll be okay."

Okay is one thing he's not. "Come home with me. We'll tell my parents. They'll call the police, and he'll be arrested. All they have to do is look at your face ...."

"Forget it. He'll say I attacked him or something, and he did it in self-defense. He's a cop and I'm a criminal. Cops believe their own," he says.

"I'll tell them what he did to me, they'll have to do something."

"I'll be arrested. Statutory rape, remember?"

"My parents aren't going to press charges."

"Even if they don't, they ain't gonna let us see each other no more, that's for sure."

I say nothing. He's got me there.

He folds me in his arms again and I suck in his scent. It soothes me a little, but not enough. I say, "I'm afraid he's going to kill you."

He says, "He ain't gonna kill me."
He says, "He ain't gonna kill me tonight."

JOEY

So she cleans up she showers off my blood and both our
snot and tears she's good
to
go.
'Cept for a few wrinkles in her blouse she looks the
same as when she came in
look at that
she passes
too.

She fixes me up too she insists even though I tell her not
to waste her time. She pats at my face with a washcloth trying not
to
hurt me
and me
I try not to show it
hurts. She dabs on this antibiotic ointment she found in the
medicine cabinet. Then she gets a London broil from the freezer
she says to hold it to my lips.

I walk her
home
icy steak pressed to my mouth with one hand
her hand in the other.
I don't wanna take a chance on her parents seeing me like this so I
stop at the end of her street
I let go of her
hand.
She starts crying

again I wipe her tears
away I tell her
don't
cry
'cause her parents will see and they'll ask
questions and she nods and she sniffs and she
stops.
       I move my meat from my mouth
kiss her
it don't hurt so much my lips they're cold they're
numb
then I say she
better
go.
She nods again and she
does it.
She heads off
down her block with her
head
down
and I watch with my prime cut of beef
against my face
I wonder if her
head'll ever
pick
up
again
I watch her turn
right

into her driveway.
>Good.
>She's
safe inside them
gates that's where she
belongs on the other side of them
bars thank god they're nice and
thick she's
safe.
>Goodnight Doll.

DOROTHY

Halfway up my driveway I decide to tell them.

I decide to tell my parents everything.

They've been better, they've been coming around. And they're shrinks, they have to have compassion for Joey with everything he's been through, right?

They'll let us see each other, they've got to. Maybe not at first, but they'll realize we belong together. They'll realize what a great guy Joey is, especially if he gets away from his dad.

That's the important thing, he has to get away from his dad.

No matter what else happens. Even if they do keep us apart.

He needs to get away from his dad, and the rest will work itself out.

Somehow it'll all work out.

I step inside my door and click the lock behind me. When I turn around, they're there.

Right there, side by side, arms crossed, glaring.

Practically breathing down my neck.

"Oh, you scared me," I say. "What's going on?"

"Where were you today?" my dad says in a quite pissed voice.

Shit! They know I ditched school. "Uh ...." I struggle to come up with something.

"We've been calling your phone," Mom snaps. Damn. I had it on silent and never put the ringer back on.

"Umm …." I'm thinking and thinking and then I realize it really doesn't matter 'cause I'm going to tell them anyway. This is just more proof that I need to. So I start. "Well, it's like this—"

Mom cuts me off. "That's the last time you'll go anywhere near that Joey Riley, I'll tell you that much." Whoa. This isn't good, for her to have this reaction before she even hears what happened. "Why?"

"I have a good mind to have him arrested."

"For what?"

"Kidnapping."

"Are you crazy? He didn't kidnap me …."

"Unlawful imprisonment."

"Do you think I was chained up somewhere?" Funny, I was locked up, but not by Joey.

I guess it's not funny.

I'd tell them if they'd let me. "Listen …."

"Statutory rape."

There it is again. It stops me; it's the one truth we can't escape. Why'd he have to turn eighteen? It's like playing tag with no safe zone.

"You're having sex, aren't you?"

I face the golden-brown Spanish tile paving our hall because I can't face them. I nod.

"Oh my god, my baby," Mom shrieks. She's practically hyperventilating. Wow, this is getting way dramatic and I haven't even gotten my story out yet. Aren't shrinks supposed to be reasonable?

My dad says, "Your mother dropped off your book bag at school—she saw you forgot it in your room."

I didn't forget it, I just didn't need it. Stupid, stupid. I should've taken it with me anyway. I'm not savvy at the art of cutting.

He says, "But surprise, you weren't there. And even bigger surprise, they said I'd called to say you were sick. So I gather your boyfriend impersonated me on the phone?"

He did. "I have to tell you something important …," I say, but now Dad cuts me off. Now, he's got a lot to say.

He takes a breath in, goes on. "Your mother canceled her sessions for today so she could search for you. Who knew—you might have been abducted."

Big breath. Then, "The people at the school said you were probably skipping school, that your mother shouldn't worry about things like abduction. But she insisted that you wouldn't do anything like that. She said she trusted you."

He sucks air in, blows out. "She looked up your boyfriend's address and went over, but no one answered." I heard nothing, no doorbell—but then, I'd been a little preoccupied. "And then she called Amy's mother, who was absolutely appalled when she heard you were dating Joey Riley. She told her all about him …." Shit. Amy's mom is PTA president, and just like her daughter she knows everything about everyone. "About his drinking and drug use, his violence, his arrests, his jail time …."

Shit, shit, shit. He takes another breath, but before he can start in again, Mom bursts in. "I knew there was something wrong with him when I saw those hands." She looks me direct in the eyes. "Does he hit you?"

"Oh god no, he's so gentle …." My voice trails off in frustration. This was just what I'd wanted to tell them in the beginning, discuss with them—how Joey could be two different people. They'd been too busy shrinking me out.

She shakes her finger at me. "Give him time, Dorothy. Boys like that, they'll erupt all over anyone in their path."

Nice of the therapist to typecast him. I want to defend him, I want them to know all that Joey's gone through, but all that comes out of my throat is, "No." That's all I can say, that's all I can manage after what's happened today. I want to curl up in a ball. I want to roll up in myself and hide, take refuge.

I can't believe they're judging Joey like this.

But why can't I? It's not like they fawned all over him before.

I was so dumb, to think they'd want to help him.

No one wants to help him. Not even him.

Mom and Dad are both lashing out at me now, about Joey. Talking over each other about how horrible he is. They don't even care why, why he acts like he does. If they gave it a thought they'd be bound to come up with some kind of educated guess—it's their jobs.

Aren't shrinks supposed to care why?

"Bottom line, young lady—you are forbidden to see him again," says Dad.

I want to tell them to go fuck themselves, but I just don't have it in me. I brush past them, head for the stairs, head for my room.

JOEY

I stare up from my bed at the ceiling. I wanna sleep but I
can't
shut
my eyes.

I just stare stare stare hoping to
drop
off.

I drank the beer I had. Four or five bottles who remembers
whatever it was it wasn't
enough.
But I sure don't have what it takes to
haul out of this bed go out and get more.
No way.

I lie in the dark
sore
as
shit
my steak's on the floor
thawing
probably halfway done by now at
least
I couldn't hold it on me
no
more.
I stare at the bare
ceiling I ripped down the poster when I got back home.
Even in the dark I could

see

her

up there and right now

I can't take nothing 'cept

clear

blank

nothing.

      That's all I wanna look at.

      Nothing.

      He came home 'bout eleven put on that goddamn Sinatra.

He's down there knocking back whiskey

blasting

"My Way."

      Jimmy he ain't home at least I don't think so I didn't hear

him. Good for him

if he's got somewhere to

crash. I couldn't do that with

Doll I couldn't take that

chance that her parents would walk in ....

      Doll.

      There she is

again.

      I been thinkin 'bout her

all

night

trying to think of a way

trying to think of

some

other

way
but there's none.
I gotta cut her loose I
can't take the chance he'll lay his dirtbag hands on her
again I gotta protect her she's gotta
go.
          I gotta break up with her and it's gotta be mean and firm I
gotta make her
hate
my
guts.
          I stare up up up at
nothing
picture life without her
Sinatra goes on and on 'bout how he did it
his way
I can't
shut
my eyes.

DOROTHY

I lie in bed, pillow pressed to my chest, eyes closed tight. Is he all right?

All the other stuff, it sucks, but it doesn't matter. We'll find a way, as long as he's all right.

I can't remember the last time I prayed, but I do it now. "Please, God," I whisper into the dark. I squeeze my eyelids shut. I can't face the night, there's been too much night in this day already. "Please, watch over him."

Joey comes into my head; I see him sprawled in his bed. Battered, alone.

It doesn't have to be this way.

"Please take care of him, God. Love him for me, until he lets me."

Ten

JOEY

Ten days.
I ain't seen her in
ten
days.
   All this waiting it's
torture
to me
to her
Doll she's waiting to
touch me
hold me
me I'm waiting to do what I
gotta
do.
   She sends me notes from school she gives them to Jimmy
she writes
one a day
I got three on Monday night.
She can't call
her parents they took her

cell
and they got her friends' parents to check phones and even double
check their cell bills online for
deleted
calls to me.
She puts in these
quotes from
poets
inventors
people that changed the world and
shit she copies them into her
notes
trying to pep me
up she's like a cheerleader for the
soul.
Rah rah
you can do it you can
fix
your
life.
      Right.
      Like you can
hammer
in some nails
tighten
up those loose
beams
like you can
patch

the rotting floorboards in your
head.
      What's next
one of those
Jesus
was a carpenter
speeches?
      My life
it's way too far
gone
for repairs the whole
foundation it's unstable it's
decaying
I can't take the chance of letting her
walk around in it anymore you never know what's gonna
collapse next the whole
ceiling might come down on her
I might
bury her
in my rubble.
      My life
it's been condemned.
      She writes 'bout AA she says maybe I could just go and
listen
maybe it could
help me.
She lists meeting days and times at the church give me a
goddamn
break

like those washouts could
possibly have
anything
to say they talk in
bumper
stickers.
          She asks me to write back
at the end of every note she
asks.
I wanna
so
bad
but I don't.
It'll only make it harder if I do.
For me
for her.
          She don't write
love
at the end.
She don't write it but
it's there
all the same.
What does she
think I am
stupid?
          It's not her fault she don't know any better what
love
can
do.

Let her go find someone
else
maybe there's someone
out there
that believes in that shit someone that goes for all that
Cinderella
Snow
White
Rapunzel
b.s.
Like that's ever gonna happen.
      Fucking fairy tales.
      All they do is mess with our heads make us
believe
in the impossible make us
hope
when there's nothing ....
      She asks 'bout my face. Looks better than you'd think. It's
one
big
purply-black
splotch like a tie-dye
shirt like the Milky Way
minus them shining
stars.
It aches
my face it
aches
but my insides

they ache
more.
I try to think
ice cubes
I picture
my
body my
head filled with
ice
numbing out my
heart my
mind.
      She asks 'bout my
pop.
Is he leaving me
alone?
      Yeah he's got other
interests to keep him
busy like throttling
Mom. Lucky for me huh?
      She asks,
How's the boxing going?
      The boxing's the only thing that's
keeping
me
going.
      She asks if I'm
all right ....
      I don't write

back but she don't
complain that I
don't she just keeps
asking me to
she keeps writing
every
day
writing
sending me those sayings and
yesterday's note it said she's sneaking
out
tonight
her parents are going to the ballet in Manhattan and she's
sneaking out to the
bridge
she knows I'll be
there it's Saturday
night.
      Tonight.
      It'll
all
be over
tonight.

DOROTHY

Such a big crowd tonight, and so loud. It's a miracle no one ever calls the cops about the noise. There's houses around the corner on each side, and voices carry over water.

But they never get in trouble, they just hide their cans and bottles if patrol cars go by, and toss them if they have to. They can be as loud as they want, and no one stops them.

When I saw the crowd, something inside me cringed, and I wanted to turn around and go home.

I wished I could see him alone tonight.

Of course I didn't leave. I walked into the noise, into the laughing, stoned voices. In a way I wish I wanted to be like them so I could do what they do and just blend in, but I don't, and I can't be something I'm not.

I'm searching for him.

I'm nudging my way through a sea of denim. Most of the faces I know and some of the names even, but I only want to talk to Joey. It's been so long and I haven't heard a word back from him. I've been telling myself that doesn't mean anything, but if that's true, maybe that's worse.

He knows I'm coming. So where is he?

I see Jason finally. He shrugs when I ask about Joey except to point more toward the center. I brush some more past bodies holding bottles and glowing cigarettes. I take in a big a whiff of smoke, cough, and then I see Jimmy and his girlfriend Shana. They say they just saw Joey a minute ago, he can't be far.

Then I find him, suddenly he's right there in my path, at the end of my path, leaning against the bridge railing. I see his bruises. Even in this bad lighting with only the one streetlight beaming nearby, even like this he's discolored. "Hey," I say, but he doesn't say anything back. I reach for him, I grab him up in my arms and he hugs me back, but it's not like always. He's stiff. There's something wrong.

I knew there was something wrong, going all this time without an answer, without any reply at all. I tried to tell myself different, but I knew.

Really, I knew all along, from the beginning—that there was something wrong. I just thought we could get past it.

But there's something in his vibe that's changed, it's holding me back even as he holds me, it's keeping me away ....

"Joey, what is it?"

Then I feel it press into the small of my back. It's a bottle. It's a bottle he's holding and it's bigger than a beer bottle.

Fuck.

He's back to the rum.

"It's nothing ....I'm just ...." His Bacardi breath blasts me then. I want to be understanding. I know he's been through so much, but the last time I saw him drinking that stuff I also saw him almost kill someone.

"When did you start drinking rum again?" I ask. Dammit, this isn't the conversation I wanted to have. I missed him so much, I guess I didn't want any conversation. I just wanted to feel him again.

But I can't let this go.

He sighs. "Lay off me."

Lay off of him. He hasn't seen me in ten days, and this

is what I get? Why wasn't he looking forward to being with me? Why couldn't I mean more to him than drinking?

I pull out of his arms.

It doesn't take much effort, he was barely there anyway.

I look him in the eyes. They're impossible to read. It's like he's closed off access, like he's changed the keycode or something.

I say, "I missed you."

He looks away, says nothing. What the hell is wrong with him? It's more than just the drinking ....

I say soft, "Can we go somewhere?"

He says hard, "Why? So you can lecture me about what a bad boy I am?"

Oh god. "No ...."

His voice is like the steel we're standing on. His breath—it pokes at me, it thrusts at me like crackling flames, like fire. I'm cornered, I'm melting from its heat.

He bellows, "Save it, okay? 'Cause I don't wanna be saved." People are staring now, between him raising his voice, and me crying. I didn't even realize I was crying, until a tear rolled into my mouth.

He says, "Why don't you go home, *Dorothy*? Why don't you go back behind them gates where it's nice and safe and there's no way for me to get past, there's no way for big bad me to get to you, to huff and to puff and blow your life in."

I can't speak. I make this croaking, choking sound.

He says, "Go back where you belong, Dorothy. You can't change me—you saw my genes—you got a real good look at them, didn't you." He moves in on me now, he's against me, his chest is pounding against mine, and he's scaring me. His eyes, they're cold and blank. He's leaning on me; he puts his hands out, he touches my shoulders, and then for one second I think he's going to hold me, fold me into his arms, laugh, say this was a big joke.

Instead, he shoves me.

I stumble back, I almost fall.

"Go home," he says.

Oh god, I want to die.

JOEY

I shoved her
it took
everything I
had I
pushed her real
rough
and that was it.
I knew that would be it.
She's
hysterical she's
bumping
by all the people who were
watching us like a
freak show
she's heading pretty fast for someone
crying
so
hard.
I take another swig of Bacardi it's only my
third I had
two so I could
smell like I been drinking it. I take another now and it tastes like
shit why the
hell do I
drink
this
stuff?

I can't see her anymore she's
gone
oh god
she's
gone
this bottle it's so
heavy
in my hand
I look out at the water
at the stupid ripples moving in the stupid
moonlight
all that water where's it
go anyway what's
the
point?
I pull my arm
back I
pitch
the rum
right out there in the
water it goes pretty
far before it
thunks
down and
splats right by a
duck
who flaps off like a
bat
out of hell.

I turn away
before I can see if it
sinks or floats.
Everyone's still
staring at me
christ
they need to get a
life I yell out, Which one of you
losers
is gonna spot me a
six-pack?

Eleven

JOEY

  The sign outside the
church
has a message posted in those
plastic
letters.
It's from Jesus.
It says,
When I was on the cross
I thought of
you.
  Say that's even
true. How's that supposed to make me
feel? Now I gotta
feel bad 'bout Jesus dying
personally
for me
on top of everything else?
  Inside the rectory there's lots of
statues and crosses they're basically
everywhere

you turn. I ain't been here since my communion but I remember
all them statues
and
crosses you don't forget stuff like that
things like statues and crosses they
loom.

     There aren't any
people
around but I hear
voices upstairs.

     I don't know if it's the
tiles on the floor or the
emptiness of the hall but my
sneakers they squeal awful
loud.

     I head through the door to the stairs. I go up up up
trying not to
squeak
but it's like I been
tramping through the
tide or something like my sneakers are
soaked
the sounds I'm making.

     My heart it's like a
sledgehammer all of a sudden
clobbering away.

     Stupid shit heart.

     I don't even know
why I'm here 'cept

Doll she kept at me to
come and maybe I feel like I owe it
to her
even though she don't know
I'm
here.

      She can't know.
      This's all
bullshit
anyways
all this AA crap but she
really
wanted me to come.
I keep seeing her
eyes
that night I pushed her they were so
confused so
hurt like a dog that's been
kicked
by its owner.

      The light it went out of her eyes.
      It's been more than three weeks and I can't get them
dark
hurt
eyes
out of my mind
I lie in bed
all day
the summer's almost half over but I

barely seen the sun I only see them
eyes so I thought,
I can at least
do this ....

      Upstairs
they got the long tables around in a
circle. Someone says,
Welcome.
I stare at the smoky tiles I
nod.

      I scrape
back
a chair I'd like to sit in the
back
but there ain't no
back
to a circle.

      They start the meeting and they go through all the stuff
'bout the way AA works blah
blah
blah.

      Then this guy gets introduced his name's Rich and he
looks kind of like
me
like the kind of dude I am
I mean
'cept a few years older. He tells this story
his
story

'bout how his family life sucked

his dad

he hit him and told him he wasn't worth

shit he says the only relief he could get was in a

bottle or a

bong he says he was arrested twenty-six times by the time he was

twenty-one and it was getting so jail was more like

home than

home was.

      He says he went to AA when he was twenty-two 'cause it

was

court

ordered and he still drank 'cause he thought it was all

b.s. all this talk 'bout

surrendering to a

higher

power

there was no way he was handing over the little control he had.

      He says it went like that for almost a year he went to

meetings

then he went out to

drink

and he figured

what the hell

this is my life

I'm gonna die young anyways.

Then one day he was walking to the liquor store

in the snow.

There was this humongous puddle of

slush at the
edge
of the curb and he
stopped and
stared into it.
　　　He saw his
sorry-
ass
reflection looking back and
suddenly
he thought of
surrender.
All this time he'd fought it and
look
where it got him.
All this time he thought it was
bad
that it meant
defeat
to surrender
that there'd be
nothing
left of him
that it'd be the end.
But just like that the word
appeared in his head like someone
whispered it to him and he
fell
into the

freezing
puddle he
splattered in
on his knees
he spoke to God he
surrendered.
And that's when he found
hope he found
faith that's when everything
changed
when he caved
when he gave up the
burden
of trying to control what he
couldn't
control
anyway
he felt it
lift from his shoulders and it all
changed.
      He says he went back
home
'stead of the liquor store that day and he's been
sober
a year.
He says with surrender came
serenity.
      He had me for a while and
damn he's a lot

like me
but he lost me with that
puddle.
          I ain't
surrendering to nothing I can't
see
these people they're wacked I think they pickled their brains a
little
too long.
          Ole God
he had his chance to help me
long ago
didn't he? Me my
mom my
brothers we surrendered
all right
we surrendered to
Pop
we didn't have no choice and
where
was
God
then?
          So now I'm supposed to
trust him
I'm supposed to turn
myself
over
to some dude that let us get

tortured?
      I think,
Get
real.
      I have to
stop myself from saying it out
loud.
      Other people talk tell more stories 'bout
surrender
'cause that's the topic Rich picked.
Me I'm kinda done
listening
I got more than my fill.
      To finish
everyone holds hands
they say that
serenity
prayer
that's stitched on pillows old ladies buy and lean against while
they
sip their tea.
Then everyone says, Stay.
And that's
the end.
I wanna do anything but
stay I'm practically
twitching
to escape but Rich he comes over he
shakes my hand.

He says he noticed I'm
new he noticed me
squirming
in my seat he says,
That was me
my first time.
He hands me his number
says to call
anytime
I wanna talk. Maybe he can
sense that I ain't gonna
call maybe he knows I'm gonna head right out and
pop
open a Bud 'cause he asks,
What did you think?
And I tell him the truth
why lie
I tell him I saw a lot of
me
in him
and that was cool but that
surrendering to God shit that's gotta
go.
      He laughs he says he likes my
honesty. He says it don't have to be
God like in the Bible he says he don't even read the Bible or
nothing. He says it's 'bout faith in a power
greater
than

me

it can be in any form. He says it's 'bout
yin and
yang it's 'bout
karma it's 'bout
redemption it's 'bout
love.

      Love.

      That word

again.

      Fuckin' A.

      I say,

Bro
I ain't dropping in no puddle for
no one.

      He looks at me dead-on his
eyes they're plowing straight into
mine.

      He says,

The puddle
it's in your
mind.

DOROTHY

I'm in my living room with Amy. We're watching a show about the life cycle of butterflies on the Discovery Channel. This is my life, my summer—watching tv every night. What else can you do with an eight o'clock curfew?

Not that there's anything to do anyway.

I spent the first half of the summer waiting for Joey. Looking for him to show up, magically appear on the beach, on the street, at my gate ....

Somewhere. Anywhere.

It's August.

I get it now.

He's not coming.

All across the wide-screen there's fluttering, colorful wings.

I say, "All that talk about butterflies being free, but they only get to live three to four weeks. What kind of sick joke is that?"

She says, "Maybe their deaths are merely transfigurations to another plane of existence, another metaphysical state of being."

I say, "I think they die. Period. "

Twelve

DOROTHY

Here we are in Dunkin' Donuts again. Around here in the summer life's nothing but iced lattes and donuts after the beach. Thank god school starts tomorrow.

All this noise, all this pink—I'm ready to scream. Why are we here?

But I know why.

Because Amy likes to come here, and she's been a good friend since Joey left. She's listened to me recite my tale of woe over and over without comment or complaint, without one "I told you so."

Because I'd rather be surrounded by this bantering and blaring color than left alone with nothing.

Because maybe I'll run into him here, it's where we met. I've tried so hard to forget him, think about all the bad things, the way he treated me. Every day I stretch out on my towel, close my eyes. There's sun pulsing warm into my skin. There's music coming from Amy's iPod, not loud enough to make out the songs, just a rhythmic jumble. There's the waves sliding and tumbling into the sand and then retreating as more move in. There's little kids giggling, squealing as they play, pure joy in their voices.

There's seagulls cawing; there's the ice cream truck in the parking lot playing endless rounds of "Take Me Out To The Ballgame;" · there's the smell of burgers and hotdogs grilling—but when he comes into my mind there's nothing else. I think of him drinking, throttling Brian, shoving me. I think of him bloody and angry, demanding that I not say I love him. But those pictures, they fad fast and I'm left with one of him holding me, just holding me. We're lying together in Jason's garage, and he's wrapped around me tight so tight I can feel his body on me still …. Every day I have to roll onto my stomach, press my face into my towel, practically burrow into the sand to hide my tears. They embarrass me, and I wish they'd just leave once and for all, like him.

I should be over him by now, but here I am on line at Dunkin' Donuts, praying he'll walk in.

Jimmy and Jason are here, at their usual table in the front room. They saw us come in. Jimmy shot me a quick wave, Jason gave a nod. I'd go over, but what would I say?

I'm staring into the grey tile waiting for the feet in front of me to move when someone grabs my arm.

It's Amy.

She says, "C'mere, I've got to tell you something." She pulls me off the line, pulls me outside. She says, "I was waiting for them to finish mopping the back room, leaning on the wall near the tables."

I shrug. "So?"

"I heard Jason and Jimmy talking …."

"Oh god, is Joey okay? Did his—" I stop myself before I say Dad, I'm honoring his secret no matter what. "Did he get hurt in a fight?"

"It's nothing like that," she says. She stares at me for a minute, then sighs. "Look, I'm no Joey Riley fan, and I think you're better off without him. But you're so sad all the time …."

"Would you just tell me?"

"Okay, okay." She leans against the glass Dunkin' Donuts facade. "Jason asked Jimmy what's up with Joey, why is he never around anymore."

"He doesn't hang out at the bridge drinking?" I interrupt.

"Guess not. So Jimmy says that Joey stays in his room, barely does anything except boxing and work—he got a job as a mechanic, apparently."

"He doesn't party?"

"No, and there's more. Jimmy said he's not supposed to tell, but Joey's been going to AA."

"What?" AA? That makes no sense. The last time he saw me was back to the Bacardi. He broke up with me because I wanted him to stop drinking.

Unless ….

Oh my god. It does make sense.

It all makes sense.

"I've got to go," I tell her. "I've got to talk to him."

I run all the way. Across the busy boulevard, over the rail road tracks, through the main part of town.

By the time I get to Joey's my chest is heaving, and I have to sit on his lawn for a sec or I won't be able to speak.

I knead into grass, catch my breath. My heartbeat slows to normal. I hoist myself up, head to his door, knock.

The door creaks open. The woman answering has dirty

blonde hair, a worn out expression and a black eye. "Mrs. Riley?" I guess.

She opens the screen door, steps out. She's slouched over, like there's some invisible weight on her back. "Yes?"

"Um ... is Joey home?"

She squints at me, kind of like the sun's in her eyes, except it isn't. Her right eye is encased in a swollen, purply mound. It reminds me of Joey's face the last time I saw him. "Joey's not home from his boxing lesson yet. You his girlfriend?"

"Uh ...."

Before I can answer, she decides I am. "I didn't know he had one, but I'm glad." She perks up a little now, her back straightens a tad. "That boy, he's been moping around here like somebody died. Come inside and wait." She holds the door wide for me. I'm suddenly hesitant. I don't like this house, not at all. It makes me cower inside, like there's a little kid in me all balled up in a corner, rocking.

But the need to see him, it's greater than my dread.

I go in, guide the screen closed so it doesn't bang.

"Wipe your feet, dear," she tells me as she heads to the kitchen.

I slide my sneakers on the mat, then catch up to her side. "I'm Dorothy," I tell her, thinking maybe she's heard of me.

There's no sign of recognition at my name. He never told her about us, about how happy we were.

He kept me to himself.

"I'm cooking dinner," she says. "Come in the kitchen. I gotta stir my potatoes."

We pass through the archway, pass from brown carpet to

green linoleum. I think of all the things Joey's told me went on in here, and it's hard to force a smile. "Such a tidy home you have," I tell her, because it's the polite thing to do.

"Thank you, Dorothy." She's stirring, stirring. "I try my best to keep it nice."

I'm standing next to her watching her stir, feeling my insides stirring too. I just want to talk to him already ….

"My little one, Warren, he's at a friend's house," she says. "And my James, he's having dinner at his girlfriend's. But my Joseph, he always comes home for supper." She stops stirring for a second, thinks about what she said. "Of course, I won't mind if he eats at your house sometimes. I'm not one of those mothers who can't let go …."

"It's okay," I say. All this small talk is about to send me out of my skin.

The screen door slams. Suddenly it occurs to me that it might be his dad.

I turn; I look for a back door or some exit. There's a window over the sink. Could I get up there and out before he got to me?

But it's him, it's Joey. His feet hit the linoleum twice, then stop when he sees me. He looks good.

His face, it's healed.

"Doll …."

It's there in his eyes—the light.

He lights up for a second when he sees me, before he can cover up.

He still cares.

I want to hug him, it's been so long, but he quickly masks his reaction. "What the hell are you doing here?"

"Joseph!" His mom says. "Is that any way to speak to a young lady?"

"Ma, I don't know any way to say this other than butt out," he tells her.

She turns back to her potatoes.

To me he says sharply, "You gotta get out of here."

"We need to talk," I say.

He's wearing his wraps, his gym bag's slung over his shoulder. He notices me looking and says soft, "I just got a job. I'll pay you back for the lessons."

"I don't want your money, Joey. That was a gift, no matter what ...."

My words trail off as we lock eyes.

He's fighting himself, I can see it.

Now, I see everything so clear.

JOEY

Here they are
again
these voices at
war
in my
head
they won't
shut
the hell
up. One's
wailing
for her to
stay one's
screeching
to make her
go ....

DOROTHY

He says, "You gotta leave."

"I'm not going until you listen," I say.

"I've got some laundry to fold," his mom says. I sense that's how it's done around here, you walk away from other people's messes. She hands me the spoon. It's covered with a white potato-y film. "You'll stir?"

I nod.

She goes.

I head to the stove, dunk the wooden spoon in, whirl it through the thick goop.

Joey grabs my arm, squeezes. The jolt when he connects, it's so strong I let go of the spoon.

I manage to catch hold again, hoist it out before it sinks.

"What is wrong with you?" he demands. His eyes are wide now, in desperation, in fear. "Doll, please …. Go."

"No."

He looks like he's going to burst, like he wants to drag me out of here, but he can't bring himself to. "Don't you get it? Pop's coming home!"

I should be afraid, but all I can register is how great it is to be touched by him again.

How great it is to feel again, to feel anything again.

I've been dead all summer.

The spoon in my hand, it's dripping potato mush all over the linoleum.

His hand quivers against my skin, I feel it through the soft cloth on his palm, I feel it even stronger through his fingertips. That vibrant power between us, it's undeniable.

I say, "Joey, I know."

He lets go, his hand flops right off my arm. "What do you know?"

"I know why you broke up with me … to protect me." I turn to the pot, dip back in, stir some more.

"Bullshit …."

I stir and stir, round and round. How much do you have to stir anyway? "Joey, I know you don't hang out anymore at the bridge."

"Got bored with them, that's all," he says, but his voice, it's shaking.

I lift the spoon from the potatoes, tap twice on the pot's rim to knock off the excess, stick it on the spoon rest between the burners.

I switch off the flame.

Fuck those potatoes if they're lumpy.

I take his hand, fold it in mine.

I say, "I know you're going to AA."

"Who told you that lie …?" He tries to cover still, but he can't pull it off. The vibe flowing between us, through us—it's been denied too long.

It's the truth.

"Aw, Joey," I say.

It's all I can say.

JOEY

The truth it's

out.

     I

stop then I

stop fighting it

'cause there *is* no fighting it

how could I not know that?

     I stop

fighting I stop

listening to the

arguing in my

brain I just

breathe

it in I just

breathe in

the truth.

     There's this

pop

in my head

and then it's quiet.

     They're

gone

the voices

they're

gone.

     Finally

there's silence

finally there's
peace.
        Finally
they're gone.

DOROTHY

He's crying.

He says, "You never seen what he does to her ... I couldn't take the chance, that he'd do that to you ...."

I pull him against me, he doesn't resist. He's clammy, damp and sticky from the workout. He nuzzles against my neck, it's like he was never gone. I gulp his scent, I hear him suck mine in. His tears, they feel so good. It's like they're cleansing away all the muck I've been buried in since I lost him.

He kisses me.

Oh god, he kisses me. It's water in the desert, it's the most beautiful thing I've ever tasted, he kisses me he kisses me he kisses me and everything melts away ....

Then a voice booms, "What's this?"

JOEY

He's got this big
smirk
on his face
goddamn
sleaze.
I push Doll behind me.
She was
just
leaving,
I say.
Pop
says,
Don't look that way to
me.
He steps
closer
closer
closer. I'm shaking I can't believe I'm
trembling what a
wuss
I
am. Her fingers they're digging digging
digging
into my sides her pulse it's
racing her arms they're
tight around me she's pressed on my
back we're basically

molded into one.

      This

scumbag

he steps

steps

steps his black cop shoes

squeak on the green.

He steps steps

steps he

squeaks it's

piercing.

He says,

Would your girl care to

stay for dinner?

      He

laughs he

reaches out

right

past

my

head this son of a bitch bastard he

reaches right

past me

like he just

knows he can he

reaches

for her he

strokes her hair.

DOROTHY

It happens so fast.

His dad touches my hair, I want to puke. He's got this look on his face like we're at his mercy and I think, my god, we are.

Joey lets out this scream like a wounded, cornered animal. He smashes his fist in his dad's face, his whole body rocks from the force, and I get knocked right off of him.

His dad goes down, blue and shining gold spread flat over green.

Joey's on him, he's got him by the throat with one hand.

With the other hand he un-holsters the gun.

"What did I tell you?" Joey's voice is high-pitched, wired, wild. "What did I say? I told you not to touch her again!"

His arm's clamped around his dad's neck. His chin's wedged over his dad's head, pressing into slick silver hair. He's got metal rammed against his dad's temple.

He's going to kill him.

"No, Joey," I beg him. "Please don't throw your life away ...."

"Goddamn slime," Joey spits. The flecks spray down on his dad, a few land in his eye. "Piece of crap ...."

"Joey, Joey ... calm down, okay?" But he won't calm down. He won't look at me. I don't know if he hears me at all.

His dad squirms. Joey tightens his grip. He pushes, pushes the gun into his dad's forehead, straight into the wrinkle lines.

"Fuck you, prick ...."

His voice cracks.

He sounds so pathetic. I want to grab him, hold him.

Maybe he'll drop the gun ....

But what if he doesn't?

His dad gurgles, he's turning red.

"Joseph!" It's his mom, back from her laundry. "Joseph, put the gun down!"

"Why, Ma? So Pop can shove it down your throat? You miss your kiss hello tonight from your husband?"

Joey's red, too, with rage. The two of them, Joey and his dad, they're pressed together. I'll bet this is the closest they've ever been.

"Joseph, listen to me. I'm calling 911."

"Great, all Pop's friends can come over and mop up his splattered brain. Less work for you, for once."

His mom's already gone, back in the living room. I can only hope she really calls.

"Don't, Joey ...," I say.

"Enough," Joey says, real quiet. "It's enough now. It's time for this all to be done."

"The police will arrest him, Joey. After all he did to your mom, to you, to me .... They'll have to listen."

"Screw the cops," he says. "He's gonna listen to me. For once, Pop's gonna listen to me." His arm strains even more around his dad's neck. " Are you listening, Pop?"

His dad doesn't move.

Joey clicks off the safety.

His dad nods.

I say, "Joey, sweetheart, look at me, please."

He hesitates, then he does it, he looks at me.

I stare into him with all the caring I have, I give him every
bit.

He flinches, but he keeps looking.

I say, "It doesn't have to be this way."

He's crying softly, tears course down his cheeks slow, slow.

I say, "Joey, I love you."

JOEY

I see it then.
I see the puddle
out of nowhere
it shows up right in my
head.
I throw myself
down I
plunge
in
on my knees I
splash splash
splash god it's wet so
wet it's chilling it
penetrates me I
shiver
shiver I
shudder
it wakes me up it brings me
back to life.
I feel my wall
crumple
then.
The wall I built for
control for
protection to
shield myself the
only way

I knew how. It sinks

it

melts

like a sand fortress swept into the tide.

     All

those years

building and

all

it took was a

puddle

to bring it down.

     I say,

     I

love

you

too

Doll.

     There's sirens outside lots of sirens.

     Pop's steel Glock it's so cold

in my hand

even through my wrap

it's

numbing.

My palm it's

dripping

in

sweat.

     It's

heavy

Pop's gun's
so heavy
my fingers they're damp they're sliding
my
grip
it's slipping away.
      I look in her eyes they're
wet like my puddle they're
shimmering they're
reflecting
colors like a
rainbow they're
shining her light into
me.
      This Glock
I don't wanna hold it no more
it's too heavy.
      I click the safety back on.
      I
let
go.
      It
clatters
onto the
green linoleum
floor.

The End

Thanks for reading!

Dear Reader:

I hope you enjoyed *Melt*. If you'd like to know more about how this book was inspired, please read the question and answer section following this letter. Further insights into my writing process may be found on my website, and on my Facebook author page.

This book came out of me fast. You might say the words poured through me – like I was their conduit into the world. Frustration came when my publisher went out of business, just as *Melt* was going to press. As a result, it has taken me ten years to share *Melt* with you.

Reading advance responses on Goodreads, in blogs and on social media has felt surreal. After all this time, the world is meeting Dorothy and Joey! And, it embraces them! Finally, they're home.

If you're a fan of my previous books, I thank you for your loyal support. If you're a new reader, welcome! I invite you to read the excerpts of my previous novels. Either way, I ask a favor of you. If you would review *Melt* on Amazon, Barnes and Noble and/or Goodreads, it would be extremely helpful to me. Reader support is everything to a book. *You* breathe life into it.

I would also love your thoughts on *Melt*. Please write to me through my website, or Facebook. I've been through so much in recent years, but it's all been part of the path. My journey down the Yellow Brick Road has been challenging to say the least, but I'm so grateful that in the end it brought me home to you.

Yours,
Selene

Q & A with Selene Castrovilla

Q: I love this book! What can I do to help?

A: I invite you to spread the word in any way you feel comfortable. Amazon and Goodreads reviews are invaluable, and any social media mentions are also wonderful. Blogging, Twitter (I'm @Scastrovilla and my hashtag is #yalit), Facebook, Tumblr, Instagram … wherever you socialize, a mention would be golden. Thanks!

Q: How can I contact you?

A: My website is www.SeleneCastrovilla.com. On the site there is a way to write to me. I would love it if you do!

Q: What inspired this story?

A: I take boxing lessons, and got close with my trainer, Joe. He told me more than once, "My dad used to beat my mom." That was sad, but a little too vague to be inspiring. Then one day he looked me in the eyes and said, "My dad used to come home every day and shove a gun down my mom's throat." *That* was a specific image that stuck in my head. He also told me about becoming a teen alcoholic, and how violent he was while drunk. He was tagged a "bad" kid – but no one ever bothered to find out what was going on inside. Finally, he told me about the one girl who believed in him, and loved him.

One night he said to me, "You're gonna write my story. I just know it."

I went home, and opened *The Wonderful Wizard of Oz* – which I'd instinctively purchased a few weeks prior. I didn't know why – but I always listened to the guiding voice in my head. The page I turned to was the scene in which Dorothy and her friends return to the Emerald City. The Guardian of the Gate is shocked to see them, saying:

"But I thought you had gone to visit the Wicked Witch of the West."

"We did visit her," said the Scarecrow.

"And she let you go again?" asked the man, in wonder.

"She could not help it, for she is melted," explained the Scarecrow.

She is melted. That line resounded with me. I wrote it three times on a piece of junk mail. Then I wrote, "Melt." And I knew that was the title of my book. I started writing Joe's story – it just came pouring out – with quotes from *The Wonderful Wizard of Oz* interspersed. The first section is called "No place like home," and we witness the father abusing the mother in front of Joey and his brothers. In "Munchkinland," the second part, Joey meets good-girl Dorothy in Dunkin' Donuts. This unlikely couple heads down the metaphorical Yellow Brick Road looking for a way to beat the odds and be together. But what's waiting for them ahead?

Q: Is there a message you hope to communicate through your writing?

A: I write about humanity. It's not so much a message that I mean to convey, but more a look in the mirror. This goes for my books about American history as well. No matter when a story takes place, what's in the heart never changes. I always ask the question, "What motivates people to act as they do?" Do I find the answer? I'll leave that to you, the reader, to decide.

Q: Who are your biggest literary influences?

A: I love so many writers, but my big three are William Shakespeare, William Faulkner and J.D. Salinger. Brilliant thoughts expressed in brilliant words.

Q: Do you write from an outline or are you a "pantser"?

A: Neither, but closer to "pantser" – except I know the whole thing. My stories leap out from somewhere in my brain, like they've been lying in ambush. They're complete, and demanding to be transcribed. The only explanation I can come up with is that they've been fermenting in my subconscious. This is quite a gift and I'm grateful, but it does make it hard to function in my "real" life when a story is so relentless about being told. My kids definitely don't enjoy it when my muse hits!

I would like to try a more civilized "outline" approach some day. I hear it works well. But whenever I'm considering it – and hesitating, because I'm not sure how to begin such a calm endeavor – a new story bursts forth, and away I go rushing again. Hey, there are worse things in life ;)

Q: Why YA as opposed to some other genre?

A: I write in other genres, but there's something about YA which particularly draws me. Adolescence is the most crucial time: it shapes us, and we carry the things that happen during those years for the rest of our lives. I have so many unresolved issues from when I was a teen, and as a result it's my "default" setting. People ask how I can write in a teen voice so authentically, and I say, "Because I'm still a teen." No matter what my actual age is, a part of me hovers at seventeen.

"Miss Castrovilla –Oh my gosh! I cry every single time I read your book *The Girl Next Door*. I really wanted to thank you for such a masterpiece! I've checked it out from my library so many times, once in a while just to skim it and feel the raw emotion of Jesse and Sam's love. It's ... gorgeous. When I finish high school, I'm going to pursue a degree and career in journalism, and write at home –like you. Thank you also for helping to shape my writing." –Samantha H.

Who could ask for anything more?

I'm so grateful for this writing life – and the connection I forge with my readers. I know I'm being the change I wish to see in the world – as Gandhi counseled. For me, that change is love. We need to make love our top priority. Love of others, love of our earth, love of ourselves. Imagine a world fueled by love.

Q: What is your favorite color?

A: Purple! I ensconce myself in it as much as possible.

Q: What are your favorite movies?

A: *Good Will Hunting, The Hangover, The Long Kiss Goodnight, Serendipity, My Big Fat Greek Wedding* and *Dead Again.*

Q: What are your favorite TV shows?

A: My favorite TV shows have all completed their runs (I don't watch enough TV to commit to new shows these days.) They are: *In Plain Sight, Burn Notice, Arrested Development, Seinfeld* and *Friends.* When I was a kid I loved old reruns of *The Mod Squad, It Takes a Thief* and *Starsky and Hutch..* My favorite prime time shows were the Tuesday night lineup of

Happy Days, Laverne & Shirley and *Three's Company*. I also enjoyed *The Love Boat* and *Fantasy Island* on Saturday nights.

Q: What do you want on your tombstone?

A: She cared. (Although I want to be cremated, so maybe it can be engraved on a statue. Wouldn't that be the coolest?)

Q: What's the greatest compliment a reader can give you?

A: To tell me that they cared about my characters.

Excerpt from

SAVED BY THE MUSIC

BY
SELENE CASTROVILLA

"It is required, you do awake your faith."

—William Shakespeare

1

STRANDED

THE TAXI'S SPINNING wheels spit pebbles and dirt as it left me behind at the marina's gate. The dusty haze was a perfect fit for my state of mind.

I wobbled across the driveway and into the marina, trying to balance with my heavy suitcase. Sweat beaded under my bangs.

It was unbearably bright, like the sun was aiming right at me. But looking around, I decided that the marina needed all the brightening it could get. Damaged boats lined the gravel-filled boatyard, all of them in dry dock, up on stilts like big crutches—a nautical hospital. Their exposed insides were like my wrecked life. But at least someone cared enough to fix *them*.

The sounds of saws, drills, and hammers punctured the air as I passed the workers using them. I tried tuning out the men's jeering whistles.

One yelled out, "Nice ass."

Another called, "Hey, Slim."

Some people really get off on taunting strangers. I crunched though gravel, kicking up pieces as I moved toward the water. Sailboats, cruisers, and yachts were all tied with rope to the docks.

So where was my Aunt Agatha's barge? What did a barge even look like?

Aunt Agatha had told me about the barges that kings rode on centuries before, but she'd never actually described their appearance. There didn't seem to be anything worthy of royalty bobbing about in this marina, at least not anything I saw.

"Over here, Willow!" a scratchy voice called out.

There was Aunt Agatha, waving from the deck of a huge and hideous metal monstrosity. *This blows*, I thought, doubting there'd be any cable TV.

My aunt hurried off the vile green vessel, prancing along a wooden plank across the water to reach me.

"What *is* that ugly thing?" I asked.

"That barge is our future concert hall!"

She could not be serious.

"It looks like it belongs in the army."

"Darling, it just needs some work."

I couldn't believe my bad karma. Instead of staying in the run-down house where I lived with my mother—that is, whenever my mom actually came home—I'd be spending the summer on a steel nightmare. At least, in the house, I had my own room with all my stuff, instead of whatever I could squeeze into my suitcase.

Snatching my giant bag, Aunt Agatha galloped back up the narrow gangplank that stretched from the dock to the barge.

"What are you waiting for, dear heart?" she called. "An invitation?"

I studied the gray, decaying wood of the gangplank, which was still shaking from her running on it.

I can't get on that, I thought. *My aunt is nuts!*

Beaming at me with her sunbaked, craggy face, Aunt Agatha looked like a happy walnut. What could she possibly be smiling about? She wore a baggy, paint-splotched sweatshirt and frayed jeans.

Why couldn't she just be normal?

"Hurry up," she urged. "Time's ticking!"

I eyed the plank again. "You want me to cross the water on that thing? No way!"

"It's the only way, love."

I didn't want to tell Aunt Agatha I was scared.

"Put your mind in the soles of your feet," she said, dancing on the plank.

What did that mean?

Her voice was bursting with enthusiasm, which annoyed the hell out of me. "Don't look down."

I looked down. *Yuk!* Could any fish survive in that murk? A piece of a tire and a crushed milk carton floated by. I shivered. I was next.

"Concentrate, darling. You can do it!"

My gaze returned to the scrawny piece of lumber. What if it snapped? I couldn't swim.

I bit my lip and shuffled mentally through my options: #1: Run. #2: Call the authorities. #3: Keep quiet and walk the plank.

If I ran away from the barge, it would be smack into the hellish slum I'd just ridden through, which waited outside the tall barbed wire fence of the boatyard.

I didn't see any pay phones around the god-forsaken marina, and I was about the only one in tenth grade without a cell phone. That meant I'd have to get on the barge, plank or not. I needed to meet Aunt Agatha's demands –for now.

She held out her hand as far as she could reach. "Come on, love," she coaxed.

I tried to put my mind in my soles, like she said. I placed one foot on the wood. It quivered. I tried not to.

I knelt and began crawling across the creaking, sagging plank. It smelled moldy and felt rough. I held my breath. The plank bounced. My eyes focused on my aunt's insanely happy face, and I forced my body to go on.

"Okay, love!"

Aunt Agatha's outstretched hand waited, just inches away. I lurched forward. The plank shook again as our hands locked. I'd made it.

"Welcome home, darling," she bubbled, giving me a hug.

Home? This place would never be home.

"And remember, things are only obstacles if you perceive them as such," Aunt Agatha added.

Everything was an obstacle. Especially her and her sorry barge.

Excerpt from

THE GIRL NEXT DOOR

BY

SELENE CASTROVILLA

"Life begins perpetually …
Life, forever dying to be born afresh,
forever young and eager,
will presently stand upon this earth as upon a footstool,
and stretch out its realm amidst the stars."

—H.G. Wells

Chapter One

JESSE'S DYING.

The doctors are 96 percent sure of it.

They even have a time-line: seven months. They give him seven months, tops. I try to hold on to hope, but 4 percent is a weak reed to cling to while you're thrashing to keep your head above water.

I caught Jesse crying one morning when he thought I was sleeping. Gwen, his mom, lets me stay over because he's afraid to be alone. He doesn't want to die alone.

I sleep in his old bed; it's on a low iron frame with wheels. Jesse sleeps in his new hospital bed; it's high from the ground, with thick silver bars on the sides and fake wood paneling on the headboard. It's ugly and depressing, but sometimes he's in a lot of pain, and he can move his bed into different positions to get more comfortable.

That morning, I woke to the whirring sound of his bed moving. Then came the slight scrape of metal as he slid the plastic bucket off the edge of his bedside table and heaved. He throws up a lot from all the chemo crap they put him through.

After, he gargled with the water Maria, the housekeeper, leaves next to the bucket every night.

All of a sudden he made this kind of wounded noise and I thought he was gonna heave again, but that wasn't it—he was sobbing.

You can't blame him. One minute he's the star baseball player in high school, class president and the first junior to be editor of the school newspaper. All down the rows of slamming lockers at Midland Prep you could always hear the name Jesse Parker. Girls wanted to date him. Guys wanted to hang with him to get the excess girls.

The next minute, he's being radiated like Hiroshima, even though the doctors said he was probably gonna die anyway.

They're torturing my best friend.

I cracked my eyes open. The sunshine poured in through his window, right on the wall of shelves with all his trophies and awards facing us. On a beautiful Saturday morning, Jesse should have been buttoning his blue and yellow pinstriped uniform, putting on his cap with the navy "M" over his curly black hair, lacing his cleats, grabbing his bat and heading into the park. Instead, the uniform and cap hung at the back of his closet, the cleats were tossed who knew where, the bat was leaning in the far corner, and Jess lay in bed, some days barely able to walk.

He probably won't make it to eighteen. He'll never even get to vote.

I didn't know whether I should open my eyes and let him know I was awake—he might get embarrassed. Or maybe he wanted me to wake up.

I opened my eyes.

The first thing I saw was the picture perched on the bedside table next to me. The photo of Jess and his friends at senior movie night last November, back when things were normal, sane. It was in one of those clear lucite frames, and cracks ran across the middle of the thick plastic, right over the faces. Jess'd smashed it to the floor when I suggested he let his friends come to see him. I didn't bring them up again, but I couldn't just stick them in a drawer, and that's how the photo wound up facing me.

I looked past it and focused on Jess in his bed. He lay with his face in his pillow—not fun for him to do. He told me once that moving after a round of chemo felt like trying to do jumping jacks when you have a stomach virus.

He was crying pretty hard—I could tell by the way his whole body shook, even though the pillow muffled the sound. All I could see of his head was the deep purple skull cap with the peace sign that he insisted on wearing, even though it must have made him too hot. He didn't need it. I didn't care if he was bald; Gwen certainly didn't care if he was bald; Maria didn't care if he was bald. But he cared. I guess I would too.

He sucked in his breath, like he was trying to stop sobbing but couldn't. He clenched the pillow, and the bedcovers were pushed down to the knees of his pajamas. He used to sleep in boxers, but wouldn't wear them with me there, even though I told him it didn't matter. We used to take baths together when we were little, so what difference did it make now?

I slid back my thick comforter and stepped onto the cold, bare wood floor. It was only April, but Maria kept the central air turned up on account of Jesse's cap. If I could've opened the window, we'd have gotten a nice fresh breeze; then he wouldn't have needed the a c. But we'd also have heard the sounds of people playing in Central Park, and whiffed the grassy smell.

Jesse never let me open the window.

Goosebumps sprang up across my body as I padded the few feet to him, past the shelves of trophies mounted against the red-striped wallpaper, and past the wheelchair, for bad days, parked beneath them.

"Jess?" I touched the soft cotton shoulder of his pajamas. He flinched.

He lifted his head and looked at me. "Samantha, I'm sorry ..."

"Shhh," I said. *What was he sorry for? Waking me up? Crying? Dying?* I stared into his eyes. Even blood red from crying, they were gorgeous. His irises were hazel, a mix of brown, blue and green. Stunning.

I climbed over the metal bar—my ankle brushed against it and a chill shot through my leg—and flopped next to him. There was a way to lower the stupid bar, but I could never figure out how. "Mom might not like this," he said, his voice sounding clogged.

"Shhh," I said again. I wiped a tear from his pale cheek. The chemo washed out his color besides knocking him out. He was so weak, I helped him roll on to his back. He winced.

You wouldn't know Jesse was sick by his physique. He'd lost a little weight in the three months since his diagnosis, but he hadn't wasted away.

Jesse's war was internal. The cancer and the chemo were going head-to-head; Jesse's insides were the scorched battlegrounds.

I rested my head against his chest. The fabric of his pajama top was cold, but I could feel the warmth from beneath. Jesse wrapped his arms around me and cried into my long brown hair.